The Grave of Lainey Grace

The Grave of Lainey Grace

AARON GALVIN

AAMES & ABERNATHY PUBLISHING

Edited by Annetta Ribken.
You can find her at **www.wordwebbing.com**
Copy Edits by Jennifer Wingard.
www.theindependentpen.com
Book design and formatting by Valerie Bellamy.
www.dog-earbookdesign.com
Cover Illustration by Kirbi Fagan.
www.kirbiillustrations.com
Cover Design by Greg Sidelnik.
www.gregsidelnik.com
Interior Illustrations by Danussa/Shutterstock.com.

ISBN-13: 978-1517046972
ISBN-10: 1517046971

ALSO BY AARON GALVIN

Find out more about Aaron Galvin
www.aarongalvin.com

for Grandpa and Adam,
my children and Karen.
I wrote this for you,
or my name is not Aaron.

to Anesa
Hope you enjoy
the read! 😊

Year 10

CHAPTER ONE

A Matter of Roses

"Think they'll come tonight, Doyle?" asked the girl.

Like the two groundskeepers she ate lunch with, the dark-haired ten-year-old wore a navy blue workman's uniform. Like the workmen, she had a white oval patch over her left breast pocket with her name stenciled in blue, cursive letters.

The girl's read *Briar Ann*.

A weathered and wiry groundskeeper not much taller than Briar glanced to the window, gnawing on his half-eaten chicken leg. Nodding, he swallowed down his food and set the chicken leg on the wax paper his wife had wrapped it in. "Might be."

Grandpa Bob leaned back in the chair next to Briar, crossing his tanned arms over his big belly. "You ought not get her hopes up, Doyle," he said, his voice gravelly and raw. "It's too early for them still and you know it."

Doyle winked at Briar anyway. Then he wiped his greasy fingers on his uniform and stepped to the office door.

Briar's heart fluttered when the Kentuckian licked his thumb and put it to the October wind.

"Just might be, Little Miss," said Doyle. "Weather's right for it."

Grandpa Bob shook his head. "There's a few leaves on them trees yet. They won't come 'til the last leaf of summer falls."

"I dunno, Bob." Doyle sucked his teeth. "Only one way to be sure, I guess."

"How's that?" Briar asked.

"Wait for tomorrow…" Doyle cackled as he sauntered back to his metal fold-up chair.

"But why won't they come until then?" Briar asked.

"That's just their way," said Grandpa Bob. "Everyone grieves different."

"Shoot," said Doyle. "You don't have to keep hallowed grounds to know that. You ever tell her about the old woman who used to sit—"

"In the middle of the cemetery," Briar droned. "Grandpa said you both thought she was a witch."

"*Thought?*" Doyle scoffed. "That there was a danged witch if ever I seen one—warts, whiskers, and all. Why, if I had any money to my name, I'd put it down right now it was her what lays them roses on the grave of Lainey Grace each fall."

"That woman was older than you, Doyle," said Grandpa Bob. "How you suppose she'd get them inside and find her way in the dark?"

"She's a witch, ain't she?" Doyle asked. "Flies them in, I reckon. Prolly puts them in a basket on the back of her broom."

Grandpa Bob took off his tinted glasses and cleaned their lenses with a napkin. "There's too many roses for one person to bring them all in just one night."

"Well I didn't say she made *just one trip*, did I?" Doyle's voice cracked. "She's prolly got them all stored up in the woods somewhere. Just flies back and forth all night long."

Doyle waved his finger around making swishing noises.

Briar giggled. "If not a witch, then who though? And how do they keep getting in?"

"You find that out, you let me and Doyle know," said Grandpa Bob. "Been trying to learn their secrets all these years, ain't we, partner?"

"Yessir," said Doyle before attacking the last bits of meat on his chicken leg.

Briar's forehead wrinkled. "But, Grandpa," she said. "You know every inch of the cemetery."

"I do indeed."

Briar glanced out the window to the cemetery's public entrance—a towering stone archway, two car lanes wide.

"And we lock up them gates every night…" said Briar.

"Yes, ma'am," said Grandpa Bob. "Both of them."

Doyle wiped grease from his chin. "She kinda sounds like Mr. Coldwater's errand boy, Ted, don't she, Bob?"

Briar crossed her arms. "I'm nothing like that grump you talk on."

"Nah, I guess not," said Doyle, licking the corners of his mouth to savor each spot of grease. "You's more like the one over yonder."

Briar glanced to her left at Doyle's motion to where Grandpa

Bob sat. She grinned at noticing they both sat with their arms folded across their chest.

"Why, lookie there," said Doyle. "We got us a rose among two thorns, Bob."

"I'm not some frilly rose," she said. "I'm a Briar."

Grandpa Bob laughed and put his thick, hairy arm around her shoulders, squeezing her with his meaty paw of a hand. "That's my girl. Pretty and sharp to boot, ain't you?"

"Yessir," said Briar as Grandpa Bob patted her on the back.

"We best get back to it, partner," Grandpa Bob glanced at Doyle. "Still got a load of work needs doing 'fore dark. Jesse finish up mowing the south lots yet?"

"Heh. What you think?" Doyle asked. "That boy's lazier than my ol' lady's cat. Paycheck worker, he is."

Briar nodded, despite not knowing what Doyle meant by paycheck worker.

"You keep on him anyway," said Grandpa Bob. "I want it done 'fore me and Little Miss here finish making our afternoon round."

"Okay," said Doyle. "But we both know how that'll go."

"Even so," said Grandpa Bob. "Keep on him."

Doyle sighed. "Speaking of stuff that cain't be done"—he tossed his chicken bones in the trashcan—"what we gonna try this year to keep them rose-givers out, boss?"

Briar munched on her PB&J sandwich, her gaze flitting to Grandpa Bob.

"Hiding by the gates don't work," Doyle continued. "Setting up shop by her grave don't work cause we cain't ever guess when they're comin'. And heck, I done already trimmed every tree branch around the wall so nobody can climb up them to jump over the—"

"We ain't gonna do nothing this year."

Doyle tugged at the collar of his uniform. "We best try something. I seen Jesse talking to his uncle Ted round back t'other day. Putting ill ideas in his head again, I'll warrant. Lord knows he wants—"

The office door hinges squelched.

Briar spun in her chair.

The man in the doorway wore the same uniform as those around the table, but he kept his shirt untucked. Black hair curled out the sides of the sweat-stained hat and he tugged its bill low over his equally dark eyes.

Paycheck worker, Briar thought, her lip curling.

"Just what do I want, old timer?" Jesse Thomason asked, allowing the door to slam behind him.

"Them alarm do-hicky things," said Doyle. "I's telling the boss you're big on installing them throughout the cemetery."

Jesse sneered. "Yeah, well that idea got nixed real quick, didn't it?" He glanced in Bob's direction. "Someone said it costs too much."

"It'd cost a man his job," said Grandpa Bob. "And the cemetery don't need them anyhow. We got along all this time with no trouble—"

"'Cept for whoever's laying them roses on the grave of Lainey Grace after hours," said Jesse.

Grandpa Bob waved him off. "They're no trouble, whoever they are. Never once disturbed another burial space."

"Says you," said Jesse. "Seems you ain't been keeping the big boss informed on everything 'round here, Bob. I heard he weren't too happy to learn somebody's still laying them roses every fall. Might be he's ready to put someone else in charge who can put a stop to them."

"I'll believe that when I hear it from Mr. Coldwater," said Grandpa Bob. "Not some pup his dog hired on."

Jesse grinned wolfishly and howled as he crossed the room. Briar leaned closer to Grandpa Bob, safe in his shadow.

"What you got for lunch today, old timer?" Jesse snatched the worn paper bag Doyle used to carry his lunch.

"Had fried chicken leftovers, but they's none there now," said Doyle. "Done ate it all."

Jesse tossed the bag. "Your woman's always cooking up something good. When you gonna bring in lunch for us, man? Better yet, why not invite the rest of us over for dinner?"

"You wanna eat at my house?" Doyle asked.

"Well, sure," said Jesse. "You eat good every day. Why not the rest of us for at least one night?"

"Okay," said Doyle. "Whattaya want?"

"Shoot, everything."

Briar sneered at Jesse's back as he took his lunch pail off the shelf then sat at the table with them.

"Ham and turkey," said Jesse. "Mashed taters with gravy, noodles, and green beans with bacon."

Doyle stroked his day-old whiskers. "That it?"

"Nah," said Jesse. "I want fresh corn on the cob and baked carrots too. Sweet tea and lemonade, since I don't know which I'll have a hankerin' for, and then for dessert I want apple pie with vanilla ice cream, and some chocolate-chip cookies, and angel food cake."

Doyle blinked. "That it?"

"Yeah," said Jesse. "Yeah, I think that'll about do it."

"What you need all that food for anyhow?" Briar asked.

"Don't worry about it," said Jesse. "When you having us over, Doyle?"

"Couldn't say," said Doyle. "Take some time to wrassle up all that food and cook it too."

Jesse unwrapped his cold bologna sandwich. "Thought your wife had everything on hand. She must have, for you to bring in all this heaven every day of the week to rub in our noses."

Doyle stood from the table, folding his paper bag, creasing the sides. "Guess I best call her and find out," he said quietly. "She might need to run in town."

Jesse barked a laugh. "I seen your ol' lady loads of times, Doyle. She don't run nowhere."

"No, she don't," said Doyle, his eyes flashing. "That's what I like about her. Don't never have to worry about her running out on me. Might be the answer to your problem is you need a big woman too, Jess."

Briar would have laughed had it not been for the warning look Grandpa Bob shot her.

Jesse stood and adjusted his ball cap. "You say something like that again, old man, and I'll knock your tail plumb in the dirt."

"Now what you know about dirt, boy?" Doyle asked.

Grandpa Bob stirred beside Briar. "Knock it off, you two. There's a little lady here with us."

"Ah, it was just a simple question, boss," said Doyle. "This pup thinks to teach me a thing or two about dirt." Doyle eyed

Jesse up and down. "Trouble is, I don't never see none on his uniform. Just how you stay so clean while the rest of our knees is covered in it, boy?"

Jesse sneered. "Guess I'm smarter than you two."

"Why you just might be." Doyle laughed as he got up and ambled to the office door. "Looks like I'll be needing me a lesson after all. Why don't we just step outside and you can teach me everything they is to know about dirt."

Briar grinned at Jesse's wavering.

Doyle turned back. "You coming?"

"Sure thing." Jesse rubbed his nose and sat down, then picked up his sandwich. "Right after I finish my lunch."

Doyle hooted then walked out, leaving Jesse to tug on his hat bill to cool off.

Briar took another bite of her sandwich, hoping a full mouth would keep her from laughing.

"You best eat quick," said Grandpa Bob to Jesse. "Lunch break's over in a couple minutes."

"It's over when I finish my sandwich." Jesse snarled.

"Not according to the clock," said Grandpa Bob. "Gives you the same thirty minutes the rest of us get. Might be you shoulda thought of that 'fore taking that smoke break."

Briar bristled when Jesse waved him off.

Grandpa Bob cooled her anger with a pat on her shoulder. "You go on outside and wait with Doyle, Little Miss," he said. "Need to make me a trip to the men's room."

Grandpa Bob leaned heavy on the table to help him stand, groaning as he stood. "Go on now," he said to Briar. "I'll be out in a minute."

Briar hesitated, watching Grandpa Bob shuffle into the bathroom and close the door behind him.

"Don't know why he won't quit already." Jesse gulped his soda and belched, long and loud. "He's slower every day."

Briar clenched her fist. "My grandpa loves his job."

"I love cigarettes," said Jesse. "Don't change the fact I need to quit smoking."

"Why don't you?"

"Still got years to think on it." Jesse shrugged. "But your grandpa's time in this job's almost up. 'Specially if them roses wind up on the grave of Lainey Grace again."

"They will," said Briar. "Grandpa Bob says nothing can keep out the ones who bring them roses."

Jesse laughed. "You know why that is, don't you?"

Briar stayed quiet.

"Shoot, everyone around town does." Jesse propped his feet up on the table. "Them roses won't stop coming 'til your granddaddy's good and ready to quit laying them on that grave each fall."

Briar felt her cheeks flush. "He wants to find out who's doing it same as everybody else. Grandpa Bob and Doyle both been trying to figure out who brings the roses since before even my daddy was born."

"Them two pranksters mean to keep people hemming and hawing each year," said Jesse. "All them fool farmer friends of theirs what get together every morning for coffee and donuts. God knows they ain't got nothing else to talk on 'cept the weather and who died."

Briar frowned.

"Sulk all you want," said Jesse. "Everybody knows it's Bob

laying them roses each year." Jesse leaned forward. "But he does it one more time and he's done for. I got that on good authority."

Briar stepped closer. "You want my grandpa's job."

"Now why would I want that?" Jesse asked. "You think I wanna be a cemetery groundskeeper all my life, you got another thing coming, Sister Sue."

"No," she said. "You just want my grandpa's house because you ain't got one no more. Not since your ex-wife took it and everything else you had in this life."

Jesse scowled. "Least I ain't no snot-nosed kid whose parents drop her off at the cemetery 'cause don't no one wanna keep watch of her."

"They don't drop me off," said Briar. "I like being here."

"*Nobody* likes being here." Jesse thumbed his nose. "Surrounded by the dead all day. It's depressing. What's a girl like you want here anyhow? You should be off playing with dolls, not planting flowers in graves and locking up them stinkin' gates."

"I like locking the gates each night," said Briar. "That's my favorite job."

Jesse scoffed, "You ain't got no job."

"I do so."

"Your grandpa pay you in anything other than candy and chewing gum?" Jesse asked. "It ain't work unless you get paid, girl."

"It ain't work if you like doing it." Briar moved to the door and sunshine. "That's what Grandpa Bob says."

"Why, ain't you just one of them hippy-dippy types? Full up with hopes and happy thoughts." Jesse took out a box of Marlboro Reds from his pocket and packed it against his palm.

He took a cigarette out and put it to his lips, lighting its end, inhaling its toxins deep.

Grandpa Bob will read him the riot act for that, Briar thought. *He knows better than to smoke in the office.*

Jesse blew a cloud of smoke in her direction. "Keep them hopes up long as you can, girlie. Won't be long 'til the world kicks you square in the teeth and knocks all them dreams right out of that pretty little head of yours."

Briar watched the end of his cigarette burn brighter. "Is that what happened to you?"

"Me, nah. I weren't never one for dreaming." Jesse took another drag. He blew it just as quick, waving the smoke away with his hand. "Find it awfully hard to when you ain't got no place to lay your head at night."

Briar snorted the foul scent away and stepped outside to the cleaner smells—earth and freshly cut grass. She felt her nose twitch with the chilly air.

Leaves crunched under her feet as she approached the wall, covered with English ivy. A teeming wall of evergreen, the wall towered near thirty feet in the air and snaked around the whole cemetery, save for two stone gateways—the main entrance to the north and the private one reserved for Mr. Coldwater to the west. The wrought iron gates hung open for now, held fast to driven stakes by coarse wire.

Doyle knelt near the wall, poking around in the dirt with a stick.

"Whatcha doing?" Briar jogged over to join him.

"Them ground squirrels is back again." Doyle pointed to a hole and the lumpy patches of earth leading away from it. He stood and adjusted the flat bill of his hat. "Looks like I'll need to get them traps out this afternoon."

"Do you have to?" Briar asked. "They ain't hurting nothing."

"So you say." Doyle pointed his stick to the main gate. "Just past that arch is hallowed ground, Little Miss. Even ground squirrels got to respect that." He mussed her hair. "Don't worry. I won't kill 'em all. If they're smart, they'll move on, once I get one or two of their kin."

"But ground squirrels ain't that smart!" she said.

"Nope." Doyle cackled then headed toward the equipment barn across the yard.

Briar knelt in the dirt, mesmerized by the dark hole tunneling into the earth, bending close as she dared. "Best move on," she whispered. "Doyle's coming back with traps and you won't want none of their bite."

The ivy rustled.

Briar sat up quick and fetched the stick Doyle left behind. Her mouth dry, she poked at the ivy with the stick's end.

The ivy shuddered with movement deep inside its hidden, lush greenery.

Briar smacked the stick against it.

Something hidden by the ivy fled in the opposite direction, rustling a straight line across the wall base.

"Briar Ann—"

She wheeled at her name being called.

Grandpa Bob stood beside the cemetery work truck. He waved her over then closed the tailgate of the cemetery's tried and true Chevrolet.

Briar glanced on the ivy, its leaves still fluttering down the row.

"Come on, Little Miss," said Grandpa Bob. "Work day's wasting."

Briar ran for the truck.

~CHAPTER TWO~

An Unexpected Gift

Grandpa Bob had the engine running when Briar climbed in the truck and slammed the creaky passenger door closed.

"What's got into you?" he asked.

"Nothing," she said. "Thought I saw something."

Grandpa Bob leaned over the steering wheel. "Hmm. Fairy, I'd reckon."

Briar cocked an eyebrow. "You really believe in fairies, Grandpa?"

"I do," he said. "Rascally little devils. They used to sneak into your grandma's garden and steal radishes when she weren't looking."

Briar rolled her eyes. "Grandma always said *you* snuck those radishes."

"Well, she said a lot of things that didn't make sense." Grandpa Bob put the truck in gear and inched toward the main gateway. "Hold your breath now. Don't want the dead stealing it away."

Briar obeyed as Grandpa Bob drove beneath the sprawling arch, its metal twisted and gnarled in spelling out the name Coldwater Cemetery. She felt the usual chill when passing through the gateway. Grandpa Bob called it the hallowed reminder for the living to tread softly.

She exhaled once they were through and then breathed the familiar, comforting smells inside the truck—a mixture of dirt, sweat, and Grandpa Bob's deodorant.

Briar would have recognized that minty, man-smell anywhere. Her mother swore the Wade menfolk kept that scented brand in business, as she had yet to learn of anyone else who used that particular deodorant.

Grandpa Bob kept a bar of the green-topped, Gillette Speed Stick inside the dash, along with a few other items: some loose change, pencil and notepad, and always a pack of Wrigley's wintergreen chewing gum.

Briar leaned to the dash and stole a stick of it then sat back against the towel-covered seats. Closing her eyes and chewing, Briar savored the bit of flavor that never lasted more than thirty seconds.

Grandpa Bob rubbed at his turkey neck.

"What's wrong, Grandpa?" she asked.

"Getting old, Little Miss," he said. "Just getting old. Reckon I'll be pushing up daisies in here soon next to your grandma. What you think?"

Briar squirmed in the seat then shrugged her shoulders.

"Ah, well," said Grandpa Bob. "Least I'll give Jesse some bit of trouble that a way." His grumbled chuckle coaxed a grin out of her. "Make him bend over a time or two."

"He'd just leave them daisies so he didn't have more work," said Briar.

"Yeah, I guess he would." Grandpa Bob laughed and continued driving down the winding path.

Briar watched out her window as they rolled past the headstones, their marbled gleams shining in the sunlight. Rectangles and squares, crosses and stars, their sizes and makes differed as much as what the bereaved left behind. Wreathes and flags, toys and cards. Briar had even found unopened six-packs sitting on graves before.

It didn't matter what was left behind, or how elegant a headstone to commemorate the deceased, she and Grandpa Bob showed equal respect and care to every burial space. And while Briar recognized many of the family names carved across their stone faces, Grandpa Bob often told her about the people buried in Coldwater Cemetery as if they were friends of his.

Each has a story all their own, he often remarked of the headstones. *Some more interesting than others, mind you, but stories all the same.*

On any other day, Briar would tease such tales out of him. But today she doubted even Grandpa Bob's tales could bring her comfort.

They looped around the western bend and Briar's gaze wandered from the headstones to Mr. Coldwater's private entrance.

Unlike the main public gate, she thought Mr. Coldwater's resembled a castle like in the stories she loved of King Arthur and his knights. Yet where Briar imagined Camelot with gleaming, white stone parapets and welcoming archways, Mr.

Coldwater's entrance gave the impression wrought iron gates were always meant to give: keep out.

"Grandpa," she said as they passed by and continued southward. "Do you really think Mr. Coldwater would fire you?"

"Oh, I dunno," he said. "Haven't heard from him directly in many a year. Don't know why he'd take a fancy to me, or care about them roses now." Grandpa Bob pursed his lips. "Don't much matter if he did anyhow. Them ones who brings the roses will get in whether it's me here or someone else."

"I guess," said Briar. "But Jesse said—"

"Lots of things, I expect," said Grandpa Bob. "Don't make them all true. That what got you bothered today? He have you worried about me and my job, or is it something else?"

Briar sighed. "I dunno."

"Haven't seen your friend since you went back to school," said Grandpa Bob. "What's her name again? The one with the pretty pink bicycle and streamers in the handlebars?"

"Emma," said Briar. "She moved to California before school started. Her daddy got a new job."

"California, huh?" said Grandpa Bob. "Well, I'll bet she's sorry she had to leave."

"No, she won't be," said Briar. "Her daddy promised to take her to see all kinds of stuff out there. The ocean and Disneyland and—"

"Weirdos?" Grandpa Bob asked. "I hear California's full of them."

"Movie stars, you mean," said Briar.

"Like I said…" Grandpa Bob grinned. "*Weirdos*. Shoot, if it's weirdos you want, we got plenty of them here."

"Grandpa…"

"No, ma'am." Grandpa Bob slowed the truck to a halt. "They don't get weirder than Doyle. Not even way out west. 'Sides"—he put the truck in park and raised a bushy eyebrow—"California ain't got the grave of Lainey Grace."

Briar glanced out her window to the lone marker atop a mounded slope. A small, unassuming rectangle with chipped corners, worn stains marred the headstone's once white face. Time had faded the birth and death engravings though many a hand, including Briar's, had tried and failed to etch a rubbing and learn such knowledge.

The grave marker gave away but one secret: the name, Lainey Grace.

Who she was, or how she came to lay in the Coldwater Cemetery none knew, not even Grandpa Bob. Neither the cemetery office nor the town library held any records on her. No one in the county shared her surname either. Other than those come to gawk at the roses each fall, Briar had yet to find anyone regular stop by.

"Why, Doyle just might be right after all." Grandpa Bob broke Briar's trance. "We get a good wind to knock these last few leaves off, maybe them rose-givers will come tonight."

Briar searched the limbs of every tree within sight, finding only a few leaves yet clinging to their wood havens. A thrill ran through her as she turned back to the grave of Lainey Grace, imagining a time soon to come when she would find the area littered with roses.

"Who do you think she was, Grandpa?" Briar asked. "Who really?"

"Oh, someone special." Grandpa Bob put his arm around Briar and tugged her close. "That much I do know. Must've been for someone to go through all the trouble of sneaking in each year."

"Think we'll ever find out more about her?"

"Can't say," said Grandpa Bob. "The dead keep their secrets better than we do. But I got me a feeling we will. Some day. Or maybe I'll just find Lainey Grace myself once I pass on and send word back to you somehow."

Briar wrenched away. "Don't talk like that. You're not so old yet."

"I am, Little Miss. Older every day." Grandpa Bob sighed. "But, long as I'm still breathing, might as well get some work done."

Briar nodded as he put the truck back in drive and followed the winding path toward the main entrance. Every so often, he slowed to a crawl and dictated to Briar what work still needed doing.

Raking leaves, pruning hedges, or else a reminder for someone to remove the fallen limbs in the south lot near the Sikes and Carroll plots—Briar swore Grandpa Bob caught sight of everything. She took down his notes, eager for the work that took her mind off other things.

They finished the round back at the main entrance.

Briar saw Doyle busy setting his traps near the ivy. She reached for the door handle.

But Grandpa Bob didn't stop the truck.

"Where we going?" she asked as he turned right out of the cemetery drive and onto East County Road.

"Need to get me something outta the equipment barn," said Grandpa Bob.

Briar scratched her head, wondering why they didn't just walk the hundred yards or so from the office to the three-story, whitewashed equipment barn.

The tires groaned when Grandpa Bob eased the truck off the paved blacktop and onto the gravel drive.

Briar caught sight of Jesse smoking as they passed.

Sneering, Jesse threw the butt of it down and stomped it out. Then he vanished deeper inside the barn.

Briar glanced at her grandfather.

"I seen him." Grandpa Bob parked next to Jesse's rusted clunker of a pickup. "Don't know who he thinks he's foolin'."

"Ain't you gonna do nothing?" Briar asked. "He could burn down the barn."

"Nah, he done squished the flame out." Grandpa Bob's knuckles turned white on the steering wheel. "But if that barn were to burn, Jesse best have his burial space picked out 'fore Doyle and me get our hands on him. They don't build good barns like this one no more."

The roar of a lawnmower sounded deep in the barn. Jesse rode out on it, driving behind them without so much as a nod or wave.

Grandpa Bob adjusted his cap. "Seems there ain't much at all in this world like things used to be, Little Miss." He patted her leg. "Come on, then. When I start sounding like your grandma, it's about time for me to get these old bones moving again."

Briar giggled and followed him out of the truck then headed around to the tailgate. She raised a hand to ward off the sun and watched Jesse shortcut to the cemetery by driving the mower behind Grandpa Bob's home.

Technically, Mr. Coldwater owned the house—a squat and single-story brick home with white siding near the roof—but he allowed the head groundskeeper to live in it.

A perk of the job, Grandpa Bob called it.

Briar knew it a curse also, remembering her grandma's chief complaint.

Can't get no work done in my garden, Bob, Grandma griped. *Not with all these visitors stopping by, asking if I know who's buried where and whatnot.*

Situated between the barn and the work office, and not fifty yards away from either, the house lived in the shadow of the ivied wall.

Briar often heard people around town called it creepy to live near a cemetery, unnatural even. She never shared such beliefs, nor listened long on their gossip. She stayed many a night at Grandpa Bob's, especially in summer when school was out, and had yet to find a single sign of zombies or ghosts.

Dead is dead, Grandpa Bob would say to such talk. *Only people that weren't kind to those now passed on need worry about being haunted.*

She quit watching Jesse and turned back to Grandpa Bob, waiting for him to lower the tailgate and make room for whatever tools they would fetch from the barn. Instead, he whistled for her to follow him inside.

A slew of barn cats skittered across the gravel lot, weaving in between Briar's footsteps, meowing for attention.

Briar knelt and swooped up an orange tomcat, nuzzling its

ears, listening to its motored purr as she followed Grandpa Bob into the barn.

"Wait here." Grandpa Bob disappeared around one of the corner stables. He returned a minute later, wheeling a bicycle.

Dents littered the frame and duct-tape covered the banana-style seat to keep the stuffing in. The handlebars had no streamers like the store bought bicycles some of Briar's classmates had, nor did it have any pretty white basket hung on the front. Instead, it had a little tin bucket wired between the handlebars and the only thing new about this bicycle was the paint job: navy blue to match their uniforms and Grandpa Bob's Chevy.

"Where did you get that?" Briar asked.

"Hazel Smith dropped it by a few days back. Said no one else wanted the danged thing and wondered if I might find a place to bury it." Grandpa Bob took off his cap and ran a hand through his greasy-black hair. "But I didn't."

"What you gonna do with a bicycle, Grandpa?"

"Me? Nothing. Figured I'd give it to you."

Briar stood straighter.

"She's not much to look on," said Grandpa Bob. "But she's yours if you want her, Little Miss."

Briar's grin broadened as she took hold of the handle-bars. Testing the weight of it, her eyes danced over the bicycle frame.

"I fixed her up a bit," said Grandpa Bob. "Or best I could, rather. Oiled up the chain and patched both of them tires. It ain't got no brakes or gears though, so be careful—"

Briar threw herself against him. Though his big belly didn't allow her arms to go all the way around him, she tried anyway.

"Oh-ho," he chuckled. "Well, all right then. You're welcome."

Briar released her hold on him and swung her leg over the bicycle. Then she kicked off the dirt floor and put her feet to the pedals, riding around him.

"Careful," Grandpa Bob drawled. "Where'd you learn to ride anyhow?"

"Emma," said Briar, her head dizzy from riding so many circles. "She taught me on her bicycle down by our secret spot. Bloodied up my knees and elbows good, but I didn't cry once."

"That's my girl," said Grandpa Bob. "Well, you best give this one a spin. Why don't you take her out for a drive while I finish up work this afternoon."

"But Grandpa—" Briar dragged her foot on the ground to stop. "What about the gates?"

"I won't lock them without you, don't you worry. Now get going, Little Miss. Make sure you're back before quitting time."

"I will be," she said. "Promise."

"All right then. Best get going." Grandpa Bob grabbed under the bicycle seat. "And keep a lookout for trolls if you head down to Newman Creek," he whispered. "You know they like to nibble on the toes of little girls."

Briar laughed.

Grunting, he gave her a good shove.

Briar kicked hard on the pedals, the handlebars bouncing in her grip as she rode over the gravel lot. She waved at Doyle across the yard, nearly losing her balance doing so. Briar righted the bicycle to the echo of his laughter and she giggled with the sudden thrill.

She turned right out of the drive, headed east, toward her

and Emma's secret spot. Picking up speed, the wind kissing her face, Briar glanced back to the barn.

Grandpa Bob stood near the tailgate of his Chevy, waving to her.

Briar waved back, already more confident in her hold of the handlebars. Then she turned her attention back to the long and empty road where the town limits ended and the country freedoms began.

CHAPTER THREE

The Last Summer Leaf

Briar dragged her feet to slow the bicycle's speed as she approached Newman Creek.

The handlebars wobbled in her grip.

Briar aimed for the tall grass at the side of the road. She swung off the side and ran alongside the bicycle as Emma once taught her. Then she gently lay her bicycle down in the ditch. Briar stared on it a good while, wishing Emma saw the gift from Grandpa Bob.

She clapped her hands then ran up the road toward their secret spot, a culvert that the waters of Newman Creek ran through.

Briar paused long enough to search for a large rock by the roadside. She kicked at one, dislodging it from the dirt, and then cradled the dusty rock in her arms. Then she tiptoed off the road and onto the culvert's metal rivets, careful not to give her presence away.

Perching near the edge, Briar listened for any sound of trolls—snores, grumbling, and the like.

But the familiar, gurgling stream of Newman Creek passing beneath her remained the only sound.

That's what the troll would want us to hear, she imagined Emma saying. *Only one way to be sure...*

Grunting, Briar heaved the rock over the side.

The rock *ker-plunk*ed, scattering the water, its sound echoing through the culvert.

Briar strained for any hint of a troll lumbering into hiding.

Again, she heard nothing.

He must be a brave troll, if he's still there.

Briar clucked her tongue then knelt to test the metal's temperature with the back of her hand. That same metal overhang had burned the underside of her legs countless times during the summer heat. And while her breath on the fall air proved she need not worry about such heat today, experience had taught her frigid metal burned bare skin near the same as the summer sun.

Satisfied neither heat nor cold would scar her with another lesson, Briar tied her brown hair up in a knot then lay on her belly and prepared herself for the final troll test, one requiring the utmost bravery.

Briar crawled further onto the overhang then peeked her head over the side.

Still, she found no trolls waiting to surprise her.

"Hellooooo!" Her voice echoed through the culvert.

Normally, Emma would be at the other end to shout back. Her long, blonde hair dangling over the water, her face a lone, comforting sight in an otherwise upturned world.

But today, Emma couldn't shout hello back because Emma wasn't there.

And even at ten years old, Briar knew she would never see Emma gracing the other culvert end again. She was half the country away now and what good was a rusty culvert compared to the sights in California?

Briar kept her stare down to the other end long after the echo died.

"Why did you have to move, Emma?" Briar asked.

But the culvert only repeated her question over and again.

Sighing, Briar sat up to the righted world and waited for the dizzying blood rush to stop. Safe in the knowledge no trolls would feast on her toes today, she maneuvered herself to a seated position and dangled her legs off the side.

There she stayed, long into the afternoon, kicking at air, staring on the creek, reflecting on all the times she and Emma spent together in their secret place. Fishing off the side, swimming when the creek was up, or the time a heavy rain washed away the jar of nickels and quarters they'd saved up from selling candy.

A few times, Emma had invited the Jefferson twins who lived down the road to play war at the culvert.

Briar hated the twins. They always tried to make her and Emma princesses for them to fight over until the war was won.

"Girls don't go to war!"

Briar remembered Tommy Jefferson saying before she knocked him off the culvert and into Newman Creek. She and Emma figured they won that war—the Jefferson boys hadn't come back since.

"They're growing up," her daddy would say of such matters. *"And know better than to play those silly games. Just like you should."*

Briar tilted her head back and winced at the sunlight.

Almost time, she thought. *And Grandpa Bob will be waiting for me.*

She rooted around the culvert's rivets, wide enough that pebbles and dirt filled the gaps closer to the road, until discovering a smooth, flat rock. With her treasure in hand, she stood on the overhang. Squinting, she kissed the rock and flung it sideways.

Once…twice…three times the rock skipped before disappearing beneath the water surface.

"Good enough for one wish," said Briar.

She thought to wish for Emma's return, but refused to waste such a gift. Daddy had told her the cold truth was she would never see Emma again. Even if she did, things would never be the same.

Nothing would change that now. Not even wishes.

Briar didn't want to believe her daddy, but she also knew he had never lied to her. Much as truth stung, Daddy warned lies hurt far worse.

Sighing, Briar closed her eyes and pictured Emma at the other end of the culvert looking back at her.

"I wish that I could have another friend like you, Emma," said Briar.

A sudden gust of wind gave her the shivers.

Briar felt terrible for voicing such a thought.

There would never be anyone else like Emma, she knew. Best friends were more special than wishes and even harder to come by.

The wind whistled in Briar's ears, drawing her attention to a single red leaf among the dull woodland canopy.

Briar rubbed her shoulders.

The wind blew harder.

The leaf stirred then fell from its branch. It swirled about, swinging like the hammock Momma strung up in the backyard, and then slowly descended. The leaf settled on the water, riding the stream toward the culvert, passing under Briar and disappearing further in.

Could it be?

Briar glanced to the other trees, her pulse racing at the sight of every naked branch. The leaves that were there yesterday had fallen into mountains of yellow, orange, and red.

She abandoned the culvert, sprinting back to the road, and leapt toward the ditch line to fetch up her bicycle. Her feet barely grazed the pedals before kicking ahead and wheeling for Grandpa Bob's home.

All the way back, she scouted each tree in search of a single leaf, finding none. Every empty branch urged her coax more speed from the bicycle.

The ride seemed endless and both her legs and back ached for a break.

Briar refused them, bursting to share the good news with Grandpa Bob and Doyle. She pumped her scrawny legs, willing them drive her onward, the pain worth it when she glimpsed the top of the cemetery's arched gateway.

She turned up the paved entry as Doyle was leaving the office.

"Well, lookie there," said Doyle. "He done gave it to you after all. How's she ride?"

"Good," said Briar. "Doyle! There's no more summer leaves. They're all gone!"

39

Doyle cracked a grin. "Well, I'll be. You be here tomorrow then to check them roses out with me?"

"Yessir," said Briar. "Nothing'll keep me from staying at Grandpa's tonight."

"All right then," said Doyle. "Your grandpa's still working inside. Out near plot thirty-three, I expect."

"Grandma?" Briar asked.

Doyle nodded. "Said to tell you where he'd be if I seen you first." He adjusted his hat. "Well, I'm off for home. You keep a lookout for them rose-givers, hear?"

"Yessir, I will," said Briar.

Doyle waved goodbye, then cut across the lawn to walk for home.

Briar thought to holler out and ask Doyle if he'd mind waiting until she found Grandpa Bob. Maybe they could give him a ride in town. She kept her mouth shut though, not wanting to offend his pride.

Instead, she leaned on her bicycle again and pedaled inside the cemetery.

The buzzing of the lawnmower echoed in the distance somewhere, but Briar didn't see Jesse. She pedaled harder at the thought of running into him with dusk approaching.

Zigzagging along the pavement, she cycled toward plot thirty-three where they'd buried Grandma.

Grandpa Bob had parked off the side of the road, half in the grass nearby her grave. Per usual, he sat on the tailgate, his arms crossed as he took in the last bits of day.

Briar waved to gain his attention and watched him lift a tanned and sun-blotched hand in acknowledgement at her approach.

Briar didn't wave back, fearing she might lose control of the bicycle for all the speed she'd gathered. She wheeled up to the truck then spun her handlebars hard at the last to stop like she'd once seen Emma do.

Her effort left a long, black skid mark.

"Grandpa, the last summer leaf—"

"You know better than that." He eyed the black mark, then swatted at a passing dragonfly.

"But, Grandpa," said Briar, "I don't have any brakes."

"Then you ought not pedal so fast." Grandpa Bob grunted as he eased off the tailgate and settled his feet to pavement. "We best get on." He groaned. "Let's load that bike of yours in the truck. We still got a few things left to do before dark."

Briar looked at the skid mark.

Grandpa Bob touched his fingers under her chin, bidding her look up at him. "'Specially if the last leaf of summer just fell."

Briar grinned.

CHAPTER FOUR

Locking the Gates

Sliding off the bicycle, Briar helped Grandpa Bob lift it into the truck bed. Then she ran to jump in the cab.

Grandpa Bob fired up the engine and put it in drive. He eased the truck out of the grass to not tear up the lawn then followed the winding path westward.

They passed a few scattered cars parked throughout the grounds along the way, just off the path shoulder, visitors who would need to leave before Grandpa Bob and Briar locked up the gates for the night.

Briar swore the truck engine grew quieter as they idled by, then hummed again once the cemetery visitors were out of sight.

"What's wrong with the engine?" Briar asked.

"It's a cemetery truck, ain't it?" Grandpa Bob chuckled. "Even this old beater knows when to show respect."

Briar wished the same could be said for Jesse Thomason's lawnmower.

Unlike Grandpa Bob, Jesse didn't bother to quit his work in respect of the evening visitors.

Briar watched him give one of the larger gravestones a wide berth, leaving near a foot of uncut grass beside it.

"Fool boy," Grandpa Bob muttered when Jesse didn't turn back to mow it.

Instead, they watched Jesse head for the exit and the equipment barn, his workday ended.

"He'll be back with weed killer tomorrow to get them leftovers," said Grandpa Bob, driving to the shoulder and throwing the truck in park.

Briar waited as her grandpa climbed out of the cab and took grass clippers from the bed.

Grandpa Bob shambled toward the uncut grass, giving a wave to visitors on their way out. Then he knelt down on the plot and hand-clipped the bits Jesse left behind.

Briar glared in the equipment barn's direction. *Paycheck worker.*

Grandpa Bob took longer to stand back up than the time it took to cut the grass. He sighed in walking back to the truck then gently laid the clippers down in the bed. Coughing, Grandpa Bob drove on.

"Huh. Well, look over yonder." Grandpa Bob pointed across Briar. "See that, Little Miss?"

"No," she said, scanning the mass of headstones. "What?"

"That tinfoil wrapped around the tin can," said Grandpa Bob. "Over by the Fulton space. You see it?"

Briar followed his point. "Yeah. So?"

"Ol' Ralph must've slipped past me somehow when he come

in to see Wilda." Grandpa Bob chuckled. "Wily devil. Them zinnias'll die soon, but the spot of color sure looks nice, don't it?"

Briar's brow furrowed. "How do you know it was Ralph to drop them off?"

"It's what families used to do in my younger years, 'specially on Memorial Day," said Grandpa Bob. "Don't see too much of that no more. Back then, we'd drive around and drop tin cans wrapped in tinfoil off with our initials on the side. That way when family would come by, they'd say, 'Ah, it looks like Bob's been here already.'"

Briar grinned. "I've never seen you do that."

"Oh, I do sometimes, when I get around to it," said Grandpa Bob. "I leave your grandma dinner-plate dahlias."

"Because they were her favorite?"

"No," said Grandpa Bob. "They're mine. I leave them just so she'd know who done it if ever she decides to crawl up outta there and come lookin' for me."

Briar laughed.

Grandpa Bob's chuckle turned into a deep cough.

"You all right?" Briar's face soured.

"Pushing too hard again," said Grandpa Bob. "Ought not have clipped that grass." He cleared his throat. "I'll be fine. Don't you worry about me, Little Miss."

But Briar did worry.

She kept quiet as Grandpa Bob made the rounds, pausing just long enough to kindly remind the bereaved that they would be locking up the gates soon.

It wasn't long before Briar found herself staring up at the Coldwater entrance with night falling fast.

"All right, Little Miss," said Grandpa Bob, turning on the headlights and putting the truck in park. "Let's get to."

Briar eased out of the cabin, her eyes glued on the gargoyle statues perched atop both gateway towers. She shivered under their stony gaze that seemed to observe her every move, daring her cross the threshold and onto Mr. Coldwater's private property.

She ran her hand alongside the truck for comfort and lingered on the warmth of its hood, knowing all the while she would have to leave its safety behind to accomplish her task.

Grandpa Bob ambled toward the furthest gate. He groaned as he bent to tug up on the wired loop that held the gate from swinging closed. Then he reached for the bars even older than he was, using them to steady himself as he stood.

Briar willed herself from the truck and hurried to loosen the other gate. *The rose-givers are coming tonight,* she thought, her fingers trembling on the wire. She tugged up on the wire, releasing the gate from its anchored stake, and then grabbed hold of an iron rung.

The cold seeped into her skin, sending shivers up her back.

She looked to Grandpa Bob on the opposite side. At his nod, they walked their gates home.

Grandpa Bob kept the gates oiled well so they swung easily inward, despite their weight, smooth and silent.

Briar waited for Grandpa Bob to close his first, backing it under the stone arch until the gate would go no further. She pushed hers in behind it, hearing the slightest clang as the gates touched. Briar winced at the sound, not wishing to disturb the cemetery's silence.

Grandpa Bob said nothing of the sound though. Instead, he took a rusty key out of his pocket, fit it into the padlock, and gave it a quick turn to the right.

Briar hurried back to the truck, not waiting on Grandpa Bob to tug on the gates and ensure them shut tight.

"You don't like them gates, huh?" Grandpa Bob asked once rejoining her and driving toward the main entrance.

Briar shook her head.

"Not tonight," she said. "The rose-givers are coming, Grandpa. I just know it."

"What? You scared of them now?"

"No," said Briar. "It's just…well, why can't they come in the day like everyone else? Why do they have to sneak in after hours?"

"Probably 'cause we lock up them gates." Grandpa Bob chuckled. "If it were left to me, I'd have them unlocked all the time. Folks have a rough go as it is trying to say goodbye. Don't know why we got to make it harder on them." The corners of his eyes crinkled. "'Specially when everyone's dying to get in."

Briar rolled her eyes.

Grandpa Bob laughed at his own corny joke. "Ah, them gates ain't nothing to be scared of, Little Miss." He placed his arm around her, rubbing the back of her head. "No more than them rose-givers, or the dead. Ain't never seen a lick of trouble from any of them in all my years."

"Then why lock the gates?" she asked.

"That's a question for Mr. Coldwater," said Grandpa Bob. "His cemetery. His rules."

Briar stewed on his answers as they approached the main entrance.

A new Ford truck waited for them outside the gates, the headlights and engine turned off, but classic rock on the radio with the volume turned low.

Briar's heart sank as they drove under the archway.

Grandpa Bob parked alongside the other truck and hand-cranked his window down. "Russ."

"Hey there." The lean, sandy-haired driver turned his gaze from Grandpa Bob to Briar. "How's it going, kiddo?"

"Hi, Daddy," said Briar. "What you doing here?"

"Seems about the only way to see you," said her father, Russ Wade. "You've been out here almost all fall break."

"I've been helping Grandpa," said Briar.

"I see that." Daddy looked to Grandpa Bob. "Awful late to be finishing up, ain't it, Dad?"

"Yeah," Grandpa Bob drawled. "Jesse ran late on me again."

"You oughta fire him and be done with it," said Daddy.

"Would if I could," said Grandpa Bob. "But you know how that goes. His uncle Ted won't stand for it."

Daddy scratched his cheek. "You think about letting Doyle take him out back?"

"Thought we might see that happen today, didn't we, Little Miss?" said Grandpa Bob.

Briar leaned across the seat. "You should've seen it, Daddy. Jesse ain't no count. He backed down quick when Doyle tried to rile him up."

"Jesse can't be that dumb then," said Daddy. "Doyle'd whoop the tar out of him."

"Says the voice of experience." Grandpa Bob barked a laugh.

"Call it what you want," said Daddy. "I ain't forgot my lesson."

Briar snorted. "You fought Doyle, Daddy?"

"Wouldn't say it was much of a fight." Daddy rubbed the back of his neck. "That geezer's quicker than he looks. Learned me not to run my mouth though, didn't he, Dad?"

Grandpa Bob nodded.

Daddy *tsk*ed at the memory then glanced at Briar. "Come on, kiddo. We best get home before your momma starts to worry."

"But, Daddy," said Briar. "The rose-givers are coming tonight! I seen the last leaf of summer fall."

Daddy frowned at his father. "You and Doyle filling her head with them stories again, Dad?"

Grandpa Bob reached for a stick of chewing gum.

"It's true, Daddy," said Briar. "They're coming tonight. Honest to goodness, I saw that last leaf down by the creek."

Daddy shook his head. "You been staying at Grandpa's almost all week, Briar Ann. Ain't you ready to come home yet?"

"I wanna stay with Grandpa," she said. "Please, Daddy. Them roses will be here come morning, I just know it."

Daddy glanced at Grandpa Bob. "You want her here again, Dad?"

"Up to you," said Grandpa Bob. "She ain't troubling me none."

Briar leaned closer to the window. "Please, Daddy. Just one more night?"

Daddy sighed. "One more night. But I want you home tomorrow, Little Miss, you hear? I wanna spend time with you too before you go back to school. Don't get to see you much with these hours they got me on."

"I will, Daddy," said Briar. "I'll be home. I swear."

"All right then," said Daddy. "Don't keep Grandpa up too late."

Briar kept her mouth shut, not wanting to make a promise she couldn't keep.

"Bye, Dad."

Grandpa Bob nodded in reply.

Briar watched her daddy back out, giving her a wave before he headed toward town.

"Okay," said Grandpa Bob. "You hungry, Little Miss?"

"Starving," she said as Grandpa Bob followed her daddy's truck toward town. "But I don't want some sit down place on account of the rose-givers might sneak in while we're gone."

"Oh, they don't come 'til late at night," said Grandpa Bob. "Not until long after little girls have fallen asleep."

"I won't sleep tonight," said Briar. "That *was* the last leaf of summer I saw, Grandpa."

"I dunno..." said Grandpa Bob. "Guess we'll see come morning."

Briar sat back, folding her arms.

For dinner, Grandpa Bob picked them up burgers and banana splits at the local Dairy Queen. Briar had hers wolfed down before they got home around 7:30. She showered quickly and then retired to what had once been her daddy's room at the end of the hall.

Jumping on one of the two twin beds, hugging a pillow that smelled like Grandma's bug spray perfume, Briar trained her gaze on the cemetery's public gateway.

The floorboards creaked outside the room.

Briar didn't turn around, even when she heard the door open.

"You waiting in the dark?" Grandpa Bob asked.

"I don't want them to see the light on," Briar whispered. "Maybe if they think I'm asleep, they'll come sooner."

"Okay then." Grandpa Bob chuckled. "I'm off to bed, Little Miss. See you don't stay up too late."

"I told you," said Briar. "I'm not going to sleep tonight."

To his credit, Grandpa Bob didn't say otherwise.

They're coming, Briar promised herself. *I know it.*

CHAPTER FIVE

Something in the Ivy

Briar woke to mewling outside her window.

She rolled in her bed, thinking to tell Grandpa Bob come morning one of his barn cats birthed kittens in the night.

The mewling sounded again.

Dumb cat, Briar thought. *Why didn't she hide her kittens in the equipment barn? Or at least wait until morning to have them?*

Her eyes heavy, Briar rolled in bed and covered her ears with a pillow.

Nothing quieted the mewling.

Sighing, Briar kicked off her covers. She yawned and sat up, rubbing sleep from her eyes.

Across the yard, the security light outside the groundskeeper office drew her eye.

The rose-givers! Briar gasped and cursed herself for falling asleep.

She hurried out of bed, throwing on her blue jeans and

donning the bulky Carhartt jacket Grandpa Bob had given her for Christmas. She zipped it up to her neck then tiptoed out of her room.

Briar crept past the bathroom, careful to dodge the wonky boards that would wake Grandpa Bob. She stalked across the living room floor and out to the musty garage, flicking on the light. Then she sat on the stoop and slipped on her work boots, lacing them up tight.

After a few yanks, she managed to open the side door. Arming herself with the flashlight Grandpa Bob kept charged on the wall, Briar stepped out into the chilly fall air.

A few stars yet gleamed down on her and the approaching dawn gave her little need to use the flashlight straightaway.

Briar crept along the outer garage, the cold giving life to her breath. Ever in the shadow of the neighboring cemetery wall, she reached the window to her guestroom in little time.

The mewling had stopped.

Briar knelt beside the home, flicking on the flashlight, scanning beneath the bushes. The light's beam revealed no kittens, nor their mother, only brick siding and a vent. She crawled along the line of bushes, sweeping her light back and forth in search.

Still she found no trace of the kittens.

Briar stood. *Where did they go?*

Then she heard a voice, high-pitched and whiney.

"Help..." the voice echoed from across the yard.

Briar stepped back, her eyes rounding at the plea. She turned her light toward the source: the lone tree near the cemetery gates.

"Help me!"

Briar gulped. She glanced back toward the garage, her mind warning she should wake Grandpa Bob.

*"Pretty oh my, and pretty oh please! Won't someone, **anyone**, bring me the keys!"*

Briar's breath turned phantom on the chill wind as it left her lips. "You can do this," she told herself, taking a step toward the gates.

"Help!"

Briar ran headlong to cross the gap between Grandpa Bob's home and the groundskeeper office. She slowed before reaching the paved drive and came to a stop altogether at the boundary line of earth and blacktop.

The voice had quit its plea.

The office security light gave her some comfort, but still Briar shivered.

"H-hello?" She swept the beam of her flashlight around, illuminating the surrounding field and office, finding nothing. "Hello…"

The night had no answer for her.

"Someone called for help," she said.

The ivy rustled along the wall.

Briar whipped the light in the noisemaker's direction. "W-Who's there?"

Again the ivy rustled.

The raised hairs on the back of her neck warned of something far more sinister than a nightly breeze.

"I'm not afraid of you." Briar stepped off the paved drive, closer to Grandpa Bob's home. "If you're trying to scare me, it won't work!"

The ivy didn't move.

"Okay," she said. "I'm leaving now. If you need help—"

"Ah, what's with that light? Ye don't need it to see," a sing-song voice rang through the air. "Over here with ye then. Trixie's trapped near the tree!"

Briar dashed to the lone tree, scanning the area with her flashlight. "Where are you?" she asked, creeping closer to the wall. "*Who* are you?"

"By the tree, I told ye! Caught like a rat. This rusty old thing's laid Trixie out splat." A chain rattled. "Bah. Can't move it at all. It won't budge an inch! Oh, it's Trixie's poor leg, this thing keeps in its pinch."

Briar crawled further up, closer to the ash tree. Taking a deep breath, she reached out to pluck back the ivy.

The flashlight's beam illuminated a ground squirrel, dead as any other Briar had ever seen, its ankle caught in one of Doyle's traps.

"Poor thing," said Briar.

The ground squirrel shivered and one of its paws slipped off, revealing tiny hands with pink fleshy fingers.

Briar fell back. "What the..."

The ground squirrel turned.

Briar gasped. What she first believed the animal's head, she now saw as a hood sewn to resemble a ground squirrel. And beneath the hood, a pair of sparkling blue eyes peeked back at her.

"Ah!" the trapped creature squealed, its hood falling off.

Briar trained her flashlight beam on not a creature, but a tiny man, no bigger than a kitten. "You're one of them!"

The little man winced in the light, raising his arms to shield his eyes. "Put out that light, now. Aye, and put it out quick. You're blindin' poor Trixie, ye block-headed brick."

Briar fumbled with the flashlight and turned it off. Then she crawled back to the ivy, staring on the little man. "Hello..."

A shock of curly red hair fell across his brow as he looked on her. "Why, you're not a creature," said he. "No talking beast, nor wight. How is it ye heard Trixie shout out his plight?"

"I-I don't know," said Briar. "I just heard someone call for help. It was you, wasn't it?"

The tiny man's eyes wandered over her. "Aye, so I did, but why should ye hear? There be none of your kind what believes in mine, dear."

"I do," said Briar. "You're a rose-giver, ain't you? I've always believed in the stories—"

"*Stories?*" the little man scoffed. "Hmm. So they come and so they go, but be they seeds of truth or lies they sow?"

Briar sat up straighter. "My grandpa wouldn't lie to me. He's told me all sorts of tales and all of them true. Nobody else believes him, but I do. Look at you. You're one of *them*, ain't you? I know it!"

The tiny man grinned. "Questions ye have, eh? Maybe it's answers I got. Give some I may, if me freedom were bought."

Briar reached for the latch keeping his leg, then hesitated. "Tell me what you are first," she said.

"Oh, look at you, lass, all wise and clever. But can't guess what Trixie is? I don't think so. Never."

"You're one of those that stole radishes from my grandma's garden." Briar smiled. "You're a fairy."

The little man's cheeks blushed furious red. He yanked at the trap jaws holding his left leg. "*Fairy?*"

Briar swallowed hard. "I-I'm sorry. I didn't mean anything—"

"Everyone likes fairies, at least so they think." The little man pouted. "Go on then. Meet one. Let ye learn that they stink!"

"Why should they?" Briar asked.

"Fairies glitter and glamour, 'tis all humans see. Ye want their secret? Fine. 'Tis naught but fairy pee."

Briar winced at his words, even as the little man roared with laughter at her reaction. "But if you're not a fairy, what are you?"

"Claim to know stories, ye innocent fawn? Then how can ye know naught of a leprechaun?"

Briar clapped. "Then you...you can give me wishes!"

"Ah...so that's what you're after." The leprechaun grinned, his face full of mischief. "*Shh!* Listen now, ye hear the tree's laughter?"

On the leprechaun's word, a fall breeze wrapped itself around Briar and the branches above her clacked against one another.

Briar shuddered.

The leprechaun's nose wrinkled and twitched. "Fear not, Little Miss. Trixie means ye no harm. Let him outta this mess and he'll show ye his charm."

"How do I know you won't run away?"

"Can't run nowhere. Not that you'd know." The leprechaun huffed. "By the time ye release me, it's three wishes I'll owe."

"But—"

"Three wishes I'll grant ye, though ye didn't play fair." The leprechaun struck the trap with his tiny fists. "But only on release of this evil snare."

"You promise you'll stay until my wishes are granted?" Briar asked. "You won't leave me?"

"Aye, I'll promise, but on one condition." The leprechaun waved her closer, whispering. "And by speakin' of this Trixie breaks tradition."

Briar nodded. "Go on."

"Ye can't wish about roses, nor to learn of Lainey Grace. I'll speak naught on either. It's not my place."

Briar slumped. "But that's all I wanna know about! Who was she? Why do you bring the roses, Trixie?"

The leprechaun winced. "Can't tell ye that. Wish that I could. For it's not you alone that's misunderstood." Trixie donned his hood. "So scream all you like, or sit there and pout. That's what me mates do, when the gates lock them out."

Briar glanced to the cemetery entry. "Your mates?"

"Aye, me and the others what sneak in our bounty." He sniffed the air several times. "They came here tonight, from all o'er the county."

Briar sat up.

Trixie clapped a hand over his mouth. "Whoop! Shouldn't a said that. Now look what I done. Trixie's went off and spoiled all the fun." He sighed. "Ah, but who cares? Them gates, they're shut tight. Though if we unlocked them…"

"What?" Briar asked. "Tell me."

Trixie's eyes rounded. "My, what a sight!"

Briar slumped. "But we can't," she said. "My grandpa keeps the only key. Even I don't know where he hides it."

Trixie waved a hand. "What need have ye of some secret key? It's wishes I'll grant ye. Use the first and we'll see."

Briar glanced at the archway and the iron bars. "You're saying I could wish to unlock the gates..."

Trixie winked. "If that's what ye want, ye must needs say I wish. Everyone knows that, ye arrogant fish."

"And then I can see the other rose-givers?" she asked. "Will they tell me the secrets of Lainey Grace and why they lay the roses?"

"Can't help ye there. It's your wish to decide." Trixie leaned closer, whispering. "But if ye open them gates...I'd open them wide."

"Are there...*big*...creatures?" Briar asked. "Giants?"

Trixie clapped himself on the head. "There, I done it. Spoken my piece. Won't say no more, until my release."

Briar reached for the hinge and unlocked the trap.

Trixie lifted his leg free and stretched it out. Then he kicked the trap closed. "So what's your first wish, lass? Your down deep desire? For Trixie will grant it, sweet little Briar."

She grinned. "You know my name. How?"

Trixie shrugged then glanced to the sky. "Best use your wish, lass, for the dawn, it comes soon. And Trixie must flee here 'fore the last light of moon."

Briar glanced to the stars fading on the horizon and the dark breaking to shades of violet. "Trixie," she said. "I wish to unlock the gates and meet the other rose-givers."

Trixie closed his eyes. His ears wiggled and cheeks reddened. Then he thumbed his nose and nodded. "*Granted.*"

Briar ran to the cemetery gates, but found them still closed. She tugged on the wrought iron bars.

They didn't give way.

"Trixie?" Briar turned back.

The leprechaun's laugh echoed above her.

Briar glanced skyward and found him sitting on top of the ivied wall.

Trixie waved at her. In his left hand, the leprechaun held a rose with petals shaded brilliant green and gold.

"Trixie, the gates," said Briar. "I wished them unlocked!"

The leprechaun shrugged. "Aye so ye did, though ye didn't say when. Can't leave that to Trixie. To him, that's a sin."

"But I wished it!"

"And I'll grant it, some day, the when at my choosing." He turned toward the other side of the wall. "Farewell, Little Briar. Best return to your snoozing."

"But you and the others are here tonight," Briar whined.

Trixie tickled the rose petals against his nose. "Aye, so we are. And them roses you'll see. But not 'til tomorrow, now that Trixie is free."

"Then grant my second wish," said Briar. "I wish to see the other rose-givers *tonight*."

The leprechaun shook his head. "One wish per year. That's all the magic I brought. Or did Trixie not warn ye? Hmm. Guess he forgot…"

Then the leprechaun winked and flopped backward over the wall, his laughter ringing in Briar's ears.

CHAPTER SIX

The Grave of Lainey Grace

"Grandpa!" Briar shook him. "Wake up!"

"Hmm?" He grumbled, waving her off.

"The rose-givers are here," she said. "I just met one outside the gates—a leprechaun."

Grandpa Bob yawned and sat up. "Leprechaun, eh?"

"Yeah, come on!" She pulled on his hand. "His name is Trixie and he said that he had to be gone before daylight."

"He better be." Grandpa Bob yawned again.

"*Grandpa!*"

"All right, I'm coming, Little Miss. Let me get my work clothes on."

"There's no time," said Briar. "The dawn's almost here."

Yawning and still in his sweatpants and nightshirt, Grandpa Bob allowed her lead him out of the bedroom and then outside the home.

"Oh no," said Briar as the sun peeked over the horizon. "He'll be gone! Quick, Grandpa."

She let go of his hand and ran across the frost-covered yard. "Briar Ann," he called after her. "Wait!"

Briar didn't listen. She cleared the distance in no time and threw herself at the gates. The cold bars stung her cheeks as she pressed against them, peering through the gaps between the bars in search of Trixie.

The headstones shimmered, reflecting the morning light that melted the icy sheen across their faces, but the leprechaun was nowhere to be seen, nor did Briar catch sight of any other creature or being.

She didn't move until a truck door slammed behind her.

"Look out, Little Miss," said Grandpa Bob, nudging her aside and fitting the gate key into the padlock.

Briar shoved open the gate upon hearing the lock click and she bolted inside the cemetery.

The morning chill stabbed at Briar's lungs with each breath. And her heart hammered against her chest in rhythm with her footfalls that disturbed the cemetery quiet.

She abandoned the paved path, weaving between headstones, uncaring of what Grandpa Bob would say of such actions, all in a direct course to reach the grave of Lainey Grace.

And then she saw it—the mound and plot teeming with roses. Deep crimson roses, orange tinged with yellow, lavender—their colors in stark contrast to the muted tones surrounding them, all nestled on a frost-ridden bed of earth.

Briar raised her arms over her head, sucking wind. Her gaze fell on the single rose lain atop Lainey Grace's headstone, its petals shaded brilliant green and gold.

"Trixie..." she said.

Briar turned at hearing the truck roll up.

Grandpa Bob stepped out, his face awestruck as he joined his granddaughter. "Well, I'll be a son of a gun," he said. "They did come in the night."

Briar nodded then walked toward the mound, carefully side-stepping the roses to not smash their petals. Stopping in front of Lainey Grace's headstone, Briar reached out and lifted the rose Trixie had laid atop it. Then she brought it back to Grandpa Bob.

"Hmm," he said, running his fingers across its petals. "Never seen one like this before."

"Trixie left it," she said. "Do you...do you think Lainey Grace would mind if I kept it?"

Grandpa Bob took the rose from her, his face souring. "Your grandma put a lot of stock in old wives' tales, 'specially the one that said anybody who left the cemetery with anything other than what they came in with, why, six months to a year later they'd be putting something back in."

"You mean burying someone?" Briar asked.

"Yes, ma'am," said Grandpa Bob, spinning the rose's stem, watching its petals flutter with the movement. "When I first started working out here, she used to drive me plumb crazy every night when I come home. Wanted me to take all my clothes off inside the cemetery and shake out all the dirt they'd gathered from working that day. Know what I told her?"

Briar shook her head.

"I said if that old wives' tale were true, I wouldn't have any family left." Grandpa Bob winked and handed the rose over.

Briar hesitated to take it. "Do you think Lainey Grace would mind?"

"You know, I think this Lainey Grace owes me a favor," said Grandpa Bob. "My guess is her friends leaving these roses are the same ones been stealing radishes outta the garden all these years. So, the way I figure it, you taking this here rose just about makes Lainey Grace and me even."

Briar grinned and took the rose.

A thorn pricked her finger as she grabbed hold of the stem. Briar winced but didn't cry out, instead lifting the rose to her nose, tickling her nostrils, drinking deep of its scent.

"Have to put a ribbon on that rose and hang it from a peg to dry," said Grandpa Bob. "If you hang it upside down, the petals dry in place and won't fall off when you put it in a vase after. It ain't every day you find a rose left by a leprechaun. Wish I coulda seen him. Rascally devil."

"He was," Briar muttered.

"Well, he's gone now," said Grandpa Bob. "And we best clear out before Jesse gets here. Don't need to give him any ammunition on thinking it's us leaving these roses."

"But, Grandpa," said Briar. "This rose proves it's not us. I've never seen one like it before."

"Nor me either," he said. "And don't you show it to him or talk about leprechauns. Folks fear what they can't understand. Only thing they can think on when something like this happens is to put it out of mind, or try to explain it away." Grandpa Bob's jaw clenched. "Don't matter what they say. You keep that rose, Little Miss, and look on it if you wanna know what's real, you hear?"

"Yessir," she said.

"All right then," said Grandpa Bob. "Let's clear outta here

then and get ready for the circus. Lord knows half the town'll be out here before too long once someone sees it and starts the gossip mill running again."

Briar nodded and followed him to the truck, shielding the rose inside her jacket as the wind picked up, howling through the headstone alleys. She climbed inside the cab, the radiator's blessed heat warming her.

"My," said Grandpa Bob. "But that sure is a sight, ain't it?"

Briar glanced out her window at the rose-covered plot.

Grandpa Bob cleared his throat. "Kinda neat to have it all to ourselves for a while, huh, Little Miss?"

"Yessir," said Briar, turning away from the mass of roses, training her gaze on the rose in her lap. "It sure is."

~ ~

The gaggle of visitors arrived sooner than Briar expected, the line of cars and trucks longer even than those that occurred each Memorial Day.

Briar stood, a witness to the same events playing out as they had every year.

People snapping pictures. Doyle asking kids not to play hide-and-seek around the headstones. A local reporter polling anyone who would reply (which was everyone) on who they thought left the roses.

By late afternoon, the lawn was torn up from all the tires and foot traffic.

"Well, Bob," said Doyle, joining them at the truck and leaning his back against it. "Guess we failed again, old buddy. Seems there's more roses here than last year. What you think, Little Miss?"

"Yeah," said Briar. "Looks like it."

Grandpa Bob nodded. "Probably cause we didn't try to stop them this year. Just think how many roses there'd be if we had them gates unlocked."

They would have been. Briar grimaced at the thought. *If only Trixie granted my wish.*

Doyle stood straighter. "Look sharp, Bob."

Briar glanced up at the sudden change in Doyle's demeanor.

A shiny black car with tinted windows drove slowly through the cemetery, the driver following Jesse Thomason's lead.

The car stopped a way back from Grandpa Bob's truck and Briar felt a stabbing in her gut when a clean-cut man in a tailored suit stepped out of the back.

Grandpa Bob left her side and walked over. "Afternoon, Ted."

"Bob." Ted nodded, then looked on the roses. "Looks like they got in again."

"Yessir," said Grandpa Bob. "Guess they did."

Briar started to her feet. "Grandpa—"

"It's all right, Little Miss." Doyle shushed her. "Don't you worry now. Let your granddaddy handle this."

She watched Ted put his hands in his pocket and give Grandpa Bob a sideways look. "Are you going to ask me what I'm doing out here, Bob?"

"No point in asking a question I already know the answer to," said Grandpa Bob.

"Nah, I guess not," said Ted. "Mr. Coldwater asked me to thank you for your service all these years."

"Shame he couldn't do it in person," said Grandpa Bob, his voice low and tempered.

"All the same," said Ted. "Wanted you to know he appreciated it. Outside of these intruders getting in every year, couldn't have found a better man to run this cemetery."

Doyle left Briar's side. "And you won't find another either, Ted. Least of all that good for nothin' nephew of yours."

Jesse stepped closer. "What'd you call me, old man?"

"Doyle, stop it," said Grandpa Bob. "No sense in you getting let go too."

Briar climbed out of the truck bed. "Let go?"

"Yes, ma'am," said Jesse. "I done warned your granddaddy not to lay them roses again, but he—"

"Shut up, boy," said Ted. "Before I have to call my sister and tell her I fired her son for being a know-it-all."

Briar thought Jesse looked like a dog run to the end of its leash.

"That's better," said Ted. "Now bag up the roses and haul them out of here. Mr. Coldwater doesn't want any more press or onlookers coming in here to stare on this grave. And he definitely doesn't want to see any roses near it."

"Don't know what he cares." Jesse grabbed a box of black ten-gallon trash-bags out of Ted's car. "Old fart never comes out here anyhow."

Briar walked to Grandpa Bob and took hold of his hand. Then she looked to Ted and his suit that bore no hint of dirt or grass stains on it. "Why are you letting my Grandpa go?"

"No, none of that now, Little Lady," said Ted. "We ain't letting him go. Just...nudging your grandpa here into early retirement."

"What if Bob don't wanna retire?" asked Doyle. "What you call that, Ted?"

"Doyle—"

"Nah, I ain't shutting up, partner," said Doyle. "This here ain't right, and I won't stand for it. You wanna fire me too, Ted, well, that's just fine. But you be a man and call this what it is. Bob deserves that, at least."

Briar expected Ted to explode at any minute, judging by the sudden change of color in his face.

"Hey, Ted," said Grandpa Bob quietly. "Tell that Mr. Coldwater I said thanks for keeping me on all these years. And don't you worry none about Doyle here. He's as loudmouth a Kentucky good ol' boy as you'll ever meet, but you won't find a harder worker and that's God's honest truth. 'Sides, you're gonna need him to show Jesse the ropes."

Briar frowned. "Jesse?"

"All right then, Bob," said Ted. "He can stay on, if he wants."

Doyle spit. "Don't reckon I—"

"He will," said Grandpa Bob. "Just needs him a minute to cool off."

Ted nodded. He opened the door to his car then turned back. "One more thing, Bob. I'm afraid I'm going to have to ask you to clear out of the house too."

Briar felt Grandpa Bob's grip loosen on her hand.

"Just who you think you are, Ted?" asked Doyle. "You gonna fire an old man then kick him outta of his home too?"

"It ain't his house," said Ted. "Mr. Coldwater owns it."

"Yeah, well Bob lives in it," said Doyle. "Raised his family in that there home and done lived in it ever since I known him."

"That may be," said Ted. "But not anymore. Can't have an old groundskeeper living on site just because that's the way things have been for a long while." Ted glanced at Grandpa Bob. "You can drop the house keys off at the office for Jesse when you're done moving. I can give you a month to clear out, Bob."

"A month?" Doyle asked. "Where's he supposed to go?"

"That's not my problem," said Ted. "Y'all should have thought of that before you decided to bring in all these roses after Jesse warned you not to."

Briar let go of Grandpa Bob's hand. "But they didn't bring the roses in! They never have."

"You tell me who did then, little lady," said Ted. "Or how they got in when your grandpa has the only key."

Briar thought on Trixie and the rose he had left behind. She glanced at the grave of Lainey Grace and the rustling bags as Jesse filled them up with roses, cursing when their thorns ripped his fingers. She looked back at Ted.

"It don't matter what you say," she said. "I know what's real. You wouldn't believe me even if I told you the truth."

"No, I expect not," said Ted. "Because the truth is there's no way anyone got in here without your grandpa knowing or helping. Speaking of which—" He looked to Grandpa Bob. "I'll be needing the cemetery gate key now."

Briar shook her head as her grandpa reached into his pocket and produced the key. "No," she said. "Don't give it to him, Grandpa."

"I got to, Little Miss," he said, handing the key over. "It ain't our cemetery no more."

Briar's fists shook as Ted dropped the key in his vest pocket.

"Hey, Uncle Ted?" Jesse called, lifting one of the trash bags full of roses. "What you want me to do with all these when I'm done."

"Burn them," said Ted.

"No!" Briar yelled. "You can't. They brought them in here for her!"

"Well, Mr. Coldwater owns this land and he doesn't want them in here," said Ted. "So say goodbye to the roses, little girl. They're never coming in here again."

Briar ran at Ted and shoved him against the car.

"Briar Ann!" Grandpa Bob thundered.

"It don't matter who's here," Briar screamed at Ted. "Them rose-givers will get in no matter what you try to keep them out! You'll see."

"Stop it, Briar," said Grandpa Bob, tugging on the back of her uniform.

Briar shrugged away and ran to the truck, swinging her leg over the bicycle seat. Then she kicked off the pavement and pedaled away, tears streaming down her cheeks, with Grandpa Bob and Doyle both shouting after her to stop.

CHAPTER SEVEN

The Secret Spot

Briar threw her bicycle in the ditch then ran down the hill toward Newman Creek. She tiptoed over the slippery rocks and stepped inside the culvert, wishing nothing more than to hide away from everything in the world.

She collapsed onto a dried piece of driftwood and then buried her face in her hands, sobbing.

"Hellooooo..."

Briar looked up, but saw no one. She glanced over her shoulder to the other end of the culvert.

Again, she saw nothing.

Then a tiny head peeked over the side, his face upside down, eyes dancing around. "Ah, there ye be. But why hide in this place?" The leprechaun sneezed. "I don't like it at all, this smelly, old space."

Briar stood. "*You!*"

Trixie flipped over, dangling his legs and body off the side, swinging back and forth like a gymnast on a pole. "Aye, Trixie's the name, and seek-and-hide is my game."

"I don't care," said Briar. "You're a liar! I don't want to play games with you."

"But games are all that I have. Games are all that I like." Trixie scratched his head. "No, that's not true. I'm quite fond of your bike." He perked. "Why not give me a ride? Ye can drive us all over. Who knows, if we're lucky, we may yet find some clover."

"I don't care what you want," said Briar. "You got my grandpa fired."

Trixie stopped swinging. "That's no fun. Why, it's not good at all." He let go of his hold and floated down onto a parcel of dried creek bed. "Come then. Tell Trixie. How did all this befall?"

Briar blinked. "How did you do that?"

"Ah, ye like that, do ye? Just a wee bit of flight." Trixie winked. "It's a secret I learned from a cute little sprite."

Briar fought back a grin. "You do know fairies then!"

"Oh, I know lots, lass, but right now I feel bad. Can't tell ye more if you're all mopey and sad."

"I am, but..." Briar looked around the culvert. "Trixie, why are you here? You told me that you had to be gone before the dawn."

"Aye, so I did. But there were a promise I made. When the others went home, behind Trixie stayed."

"I don't understand," said Briar.

"Stay near your side, 'til all your three wishes be granted. Leave before then..." His face puckered. "I'd be disenchanted."

Briar grinned. "You're going to stay with me then? Until next year when the roses come again?"

"Aye, I'll stay with ye, but first I set down some rules. You're the lone one can see me. Not the rest of them fools."

Briar chuckled. "What should we do first?"

"Whatever ye want, lass. Aye, whatever ye like. But leave it to Trixie"—the leprechaun cocked an eyebrow—"and he'll head for that bike."

"You used that rhyme already," said Briar.

Trixie yanked his hood over his face and grunted. "That's why we lepers should ne'er have to rhyme, for 'tis people like you that keep track all the time."

"I-I didn't mean anything bad by it," she said.

The leprechaun lifted his hood then dashed away, laughing a high-pitched giggle. He leapt from stone to stone over the creek water, faster than Briar's eyes followed.

"Trixie, wait!" Briar chased after him as the leprechaun disappeared into the brush, swaying the tall grass as he sprinted for her ditch line.

By the time Briar reached her bicycle, she found Trixie waiting in the little tin bucket between the handlebars, his ground squirrel hood donned, his eyes gleaming.

"Come on, Little Briar, to adventure and more! Who knows what awaits us, out there to explore?"

Briar smiled as she lifted the bicycle, watching Trixie fall against the bucket side. Then she swung her leg over the seat and kicked at the pedal.

Trixie crowed at the sudden gust of wind from their speed.

Briar cheered with him, all her worries of Grandpa Bob and the cemetery stolen away as she pedaled down the road.

Year 11

CHAPTER EIGHT

The Complex Troll

Briar swung off the bicycle outside Grandpa Bob's apartment and tied it off at the aluminum rack.

Finishing, she stepped back and stared on the ugly, four-storied apartment complex. It had once been the YMCA building before some big city man came and bought it up, renovating it as a home for old people to die in.

Or at least that's what Grandpa Bob said of his new digs.

Briar walked inside, snorting at the chlorine scent that permeated the building, despite the pool having been torn out. She waved hello to the on-duty security guard who had a belly even bigger than Grandpa Bob's, and then ran up the steps to the third floor.

She tread up the long hall, ignoring the barking dogs in 302, and plugged her nose to keep out God only knew what odor it was drifting from under the door of 309.

Briar stopped in front of room 316 and gave it her familiar knock.

Rat-tat-a-ta-tat-tat. Tat. Tat.

The next-door neighbor's door opened as far as the security chain would allow. An old woman with untamed hair and dressed in a pink muu-muu, peered down her bifocals at Briar.

"Hi, Ms. Fraufenfelder," said Briar.

The crazed woman slammed her door.

Briar sighed and rocked on her heels in wait for Grandpa Bob.

His door opened a minute later. "Well, hey there," he said, his voice even deeper than usual.

"You just wake up?" she asked.

Grandpa Bob ran his fingers through his greasy, black hair. "Just fell asleep in the chair again. Come on in, kiddo"—he motioned toward his neighbor's door—"'fore Ms. Fraufenfelder casts a spell on you."

Briar giggled. She lunged across the door, throwing her arms around Grandpa Bob, bathing in his minty Gillette Speed Stick smell. "Hi, Grandpa."

"Hey, Little Miss." Grandpa Bob gave her a squeeze. "Missed you the other day."

Briar blushed. "Sorry. Me and my friend were playing down at our secret spot."

"Oh, yeah. Remember you saying something about a new friend," said Grandpa Bob. "What was her name again?"

"*His* name." Briar strained to keep back her smirk. "And it's Trixie."

"A boy named Trixie." Grandpa Bob grunted. "Never thought I'd see the day, I'll tell you that. Everybody's so caught up in being different now they done lost their minds."

"Yeah, I guess so," said Briar.

Grandpa Bob stepped aside and waved her in. "Well, come on in, Little Miss. You want something to drink? Got some of that sweet tea in the fridge. Ain't as good as your grandma used to make, but I tolerate it."

"Sure," she said, following him inside the one-bedroom apartment.

Grandpa Bob had kept all his staple items: his worn recliner, the musty couch, and a painting of a countryside dirt road with paint flecks chipping off it. There was always a stick of butter on the table too—the real kind of butter, not the plastic margarine stuff they sell nowadays, as Grandpa Bob would say.

Briar squinted to see better. "Why's it so dark in here, Grandpa?"

"Don't like the glare on the TV."

That's an excuse. Briar thought, scarcely recalling a time she'd visited him since moving in when the shades weren't drawn.

Per usual, he had a western playing. Today he watched *The Shootist* but a whole John Wayne collection was stacked beside the TV.

"Don't you ever get tired of this one?" Briar asked, plopping on the musty, hard couch, listening to him shuffle around the tiny kitchen.

"No one gets tired of The Duke," said Grandpa Bob.

Briar didn't tell him she was. She glanced around the meager room, not for the first time wondering why he kept the stationary exercise bicycle. It had more dust on the fan wheel than anything else in the apartment.

Grandpa Bob limped back into the family room, holding a couple glasses and a metal pitcher.

"So, what you been up to?" He asked as he poured her a glass of sweet tea.

Briar shrugged then took a sip. Her face soured and she spit it back into the glass when Grandpa Bob turned to find his chair.

Easing down, he fell into it at the last, wincing.

"You okay, Grandpa?" Briar asked.

"These old knees," he said. "You been out to the cemetery lately?"

"Yessir," said Briar. "Jesse ran me out a few times when I stopped by to water the flowers on your friend's graves."

"Now why'd he go off and do something like that?"

Briar shrugged. "Said I'm just a kid. Shouldn't be allowed in without an adult on account of I might get hurt or knock over a headstone."

"Ain't right," said Grandpa Bob. "People should be allowed to come and go as they please. Shouldn't be barring folks, 'specially them ones like you who's trying to help."

Briar nodded and fiddled with the ends of her shirt as the movie played on, her thoughts drifting to Trixie and the games they would play at Newman Creek.

"Hey!" Grandpa Bob sat up as the movie credits rolled. "You wanna see what I got the other day?"

Briar straightened. "Sure."

"Wait there," he said, struggling to rise up out of his puffy chair.

Briar stood. "You need help?"

Grandpa Bob waved her off. He dabbed at his forehead then wandered around the corner to the lone bedroom. He shuffled back into the family room not a minute later with a beat up, wooden apple crate.

"What you got in there?" Briar asked.

"Oh, something I got from the cemetery the other day."

Briar blinked. "You went—"

"Heh," said Grandpa Bob. "You ain't the only one who can sneak inside without Jesse knowing. That boy's like clockwork when it comes to his bathroom breaks. Sits down every morning about ten o'clock and don't come back out for twenty minutes. Then he heads out to the equipment barn to tinker for another twenty minutes or so."

"You don't miss nothing do you, Grandpa?"

"Oh, I dunno about that," he said.

Briar rolled her eyes and leaned forward. "So what'd you get?"

"Here." Grandpa Bob placed the crate in front of her. "See for yourself."

Briar reached for the lid, its hinges opening easily. Inside, a pile of wood shavings and flower bulbs that looked like dirtied yams were covered by stained towels to keep them from falling out the gaps in the wood slats.

"What kind are they?" she asked.

"Dinner-plate dahlias," said Grandpa Bob. "Used to order them outta the catalogue every year. They die in the fall, but I'd always go out and dig some of them bulbs up and save them through winter to plant again in the spring. Save money that way." He shrugged. "And they're my favorite."

"Neat." Briar closed the lid.

"You's as bad a liar as Doyle." Grandpa Bob laughed, taking back the box. "Oh, I guess it bores younger minds, but it kept me busy once. Sure wish I coulda had time to dig up some more though." He grimaced and held up his hands for her to see. "These big mitts of mine don't work like they used to."

Briar frowned at his melancholy tone.

Grandpa Bob patted her leg. "You about ready to go, Little Miss?"

"Where?" she asked.

"Oh, don't you worry yourself about that," said Grandpa Bob. "Got something special cooked up tonight. You game?"

"Yep." Briar started for the door.

"Hold on now," said Grandpa Bob. "Have to get my keys first."

"I'll get them," she said quickly. "Where are they?"

"In there, hanging on a hook by the fridge."

Briar dashed into the kitchen. She found the keys easy enough, but the pictures on the fridge door gave her pause. One was a picture of her and Doyle in the equipment barn, him giving her bunny ears without her knowing.

Briar chuckled at the photo and her eyes wandered over all the others—her dad and his brothers standing in front of the equipment barn, Briar and all her cousins at Christmas, a teen-aged Grandpa Bob and one of his brother-in-laws seated in an army jeep.

One of a sandy-haired teenager, skinnier even than Doyle, drew Briar's eye.

He was seated on the hood of a bright red car, parked just outside the cemetery gates. The younger version of Daddy grinned broadly back at her, his dimples big and deep.

Briar took the picture off the fridge and touched the yellow-stained edges of the photo.

"A '67 Chevelle—"

Briar glanced up.

"Your daddy's first car." Grandpa Bob walked over. "Looks prouder than a peacock, don't he?"

"Yessir," she said.

Grandpa Bob smiled as he took the picture and brought it closer to his eyes.

"He looks like he's my age in that picture," said Briar.

"Nah, he was sixteen then," said Grandpa Bob. "This was a good day right here. Proud of him."

He handed the picture back to Briar.

"Can I keep it?" she asked.

"Don't see why not," he said. "You find them keys?"

Briar tucked the picture in her back pocket then snagged the keys off the hook by the fridge. "Yep. Just did."

"All right then," said Grandpa Bob. "Run on down to the truck and get your bicycle unhooked. I got to get my work cap on."

"You don't want me to wait on you?"

"Nah," he said. "Want you to go down there and time me."

Briar laughed as his big belly shook with his deep chuckle.

"Get on now," he said. "I'll be down in a minute."

CHAPTER NINE

A Fool's Feast

Five minutes, Briar thought as Grandpa Bob ambled out of the apartment complex.

Briar stood beside his Chevrolet with her bicycle already unhooked and ready to go.

"Climb up in there." He motioned to the truck bed, taking hold of the bicycle frame. "Guess you can help me out now that I'm just an old man."

Briar obliged him, heaving on the handlebars when Grandpa Bob lifted it. She leapt over the side then waited for Grandpa Bob to lean across the seat and unlock her door.

The lock popped open and the hinges screamed when she opened the door to climb in. Though Grandpa Bob kept the inside clean as ever, no towels lined the seats anymore and Briar squirmed at the unfamiliar leather touching the backs of her arms. "So where we going?"

"Patience, child," Grandpa Bob drawled and pushed his glasses up.

Briar laughed at the Wade family mantra that none of them abided. She held her breath as they drove out of the complex, wondering which direction Grandpa Bob would turn.

Right, toward the outskirts of town where all the good restaurants and shops are? she debated. *Or else left for the interstate and fast food?*

Grandpa Bob went straight.

"You ain't gonna tell me nothing?" Briar asked.

"You'll see."

Briar glanced out the window as they cut down private streets, passing her school, and the community park.

But Grandpa Bob never slowed.

Briar gave up her questions the further they drove out of town. A pit in her stomach flared once Grandpa Bob drove past the drive-in movie theatre.

"Grandpa," she said. "Daddy told me I weren't never to come this far out. Not without him."

"It's all right, Little Miss," said Grandpa Bob. "I told him where we were headed. He's gonna meet us over there."

Still, Briar fidgeted when Grandpa Bob turned in the driveway of a home near falling in on itself.

Garbage and junk, rusted semi trailers and abandoned cars, littered the neighboring yards, all overtaken by weeds and tall grass.

Not so the lawn where Grandpa Bob parked. Trimmed and well maintained, Briar nonetheless hesitated to follow him out of the truck.

"Come on, Little Miss," he said.

Briar shrunk at a guard dog's barking from some neighbor's yard. She supposed it a big dog too, to judge the sound of him.

"Grandpa, I don't like it here," she said. "I wanna go home."

The crunch of gravel bid her glance out the back window and Briar saw her daddy's truck park behind Grandpa Bob's.

Briar leapt out of Grandpa Bob's truck and ran to Daddy's side as he got out and slammed his door shut.

"Hey, Little Miss," he said. "What's got you bothered?"

The dog barked again and Briar hugged Daddy closer.

"I don't wanna stay here," she said. "I—"

"It's all right," said Daddy, rubbing her back. "That dog ain't gonna hurt you."

A screen door smacked against wooden siding near the house.

"Well, hey there, friends!"

Briar glanced to the porch.

Doyle stood on the porch, his face freshly shaved and what little hair remained on his head combed back. He was dressed in his Sunday best, though he didn't quite fill out the faded grey suit and the off-white button-up wore a stain or two. Doyle beamed as he stepped off the porch.

"Don't you worry about ol' Shadow next door now, Little Miss," said Doyle. "He looks scary, but he ain't got no real fight in him."

Briar glanced at Grandpa Bob. *"This is Doyle's house?"* she hissed.

"Yes, ma'am. Been invited for supper. You remember your manners now." Grandpa Bob started up the cracked cement walkway toward the house.

"Daddy," Briar turned and whispered. "Why didn't you tell me Doyle lived all the way out here?"

"I didn't know he did," said Daddy, taking her by the hand and following Grandpa Bob. "This is my first time visiting here too."

They approached the ramshackle home and Briar watched moths flutter around the security light that kicked on with the coming twilight.

"Thanks for coming out." Doyle greeted all three Wades with an iron handshake. "The missus and I are right tickled to have y'all. We don't never have company to speak of."

"Where's the honored guest?" Grandpa Bob asked.

Doyle grinned. "Oh, he ain't here yet."

"Late as usual, I guess."

"Yessir," said Doyle, turning back to his home. "Well, come on in now. The missus'll chew my ear off if she finds out I kept y'all out here on the porch with the cold coming on."

The steps leading into the house popped under Grandpa Bob's weight.

Briar jumped at the noise, then laughed her fright away at the face Daddy made.

Grandpa Bob wiped the bottoms of his shoes on the worn and patchy doormat before venturing inside.

Briar followed suit, then stepped into Doyle's home. Though sparsely decorated with stained furniture that looked plucked off the side of the road, Briar found the house uncommonly clean. *Momma better never come here,* she thought. *Doyle's wife'd put her cleaning skills to shame.*

Briar's stomach moaned with the uncountable scents wafting

through Doyle's home. Her shoes clacked on the chipped tile floor as she followed them into the kitchen.

"This here's my wife, Charlene," said Doyle, slipping his arm around the waist of a heavyset woman by the kitchen stove.

"Stop it, Doyle." Charlene slapped his hand away. "Don't wanna run our company off on account of you getting fresh."

Briar giggled then allowed her gaze to explore the linoleum countertops of plated desserts. Steaming apple pie, angel food cake with pink icing, chocolate chip cookies—Briar's eyes tracked them down the line, her mouth watering.

Doyle led them to a table dressed in a moth-eaten tablecloth, the metal foldout chairs bearing the name Coldwater Cemetery in black spray-painted letters across their backs.

The table dipped in the middle under all the food upon it: a glazed ham with pineapple slices, turkey and noodles, mashed potatoes and gravy, green beans with bacon, and pitchers of sweet tea and lemonade.

"Well, look at how round her eyes went, Bob." Doyle laughed. "Don't you feed her, Russ?"

"We do," said Daddy. "Only I don't think she's seen this much food, outside of Thanksgiving and Christmas dinner. Have you, kiddo?"

Briar shook her head and sat between Grandpa Bob and Daddy, not knowing what to say.

"Awfully kind of you to fix all this up for us, Charlene," said Grandpa Bob.

Doyle scoffed. "She didn't fix this up for you, Bob."

"*Doyle!*" His wife scolded.

"What?" he asked. "It's true. Don't get me wrong, we's glad to have ya'll here, but they's another guest I's waiting on."

Charlene picked up the sweet tea pitcher and poured a glass for Grandpa Bob. "Don't mind Doyle," she said.

"We don't," said Daddy.

"See," said Doyle to his wife. "They know he's got it coming. Been waiting to give this here lesson a long while, ain't we, Bob?"

"Why'd you wait so long then?" Briar asked.

Daddy pinched her.

"Ow." She jumped. "What was that for?"

"Seems you need a lesson in manners too," said Daddy.

Doyle laughed and waved them off. "Oh, it's just kids, Russ. She didn't mean nothing by it."

"All the same," said Daddy. "She knows better."

Briar shifted as Charlene picked up her glass.

"Would you like lemonade or sweet tea, honey?" Charlene asked.

"Tea, please," said Briar softly, glancing up at Daddy when he put his arm around her chair.

"Hot dog!" Doyle slapped the table, startling Briar. "Why, I think he's here."

The wiry Kentuckian jumped to his feet as Briar noticed a pair of headlights outside.

"Y'all get ready," said Doyle, a crooked grin dawning. "This is fixin' to be good."

Briar thought he lit out of the kitchen with the speed of a man half his age.

"Long as I live, I'll never understand how I put up with that man," said Charlene.

"You are a saint, Charlene," said Grandpa Bob before sipping on his sweet tea. "I've always said that."

The big woman sighed. "My own fault, I reckon. Momma always told me, 'You lay down with dogs, Charlene, you end up with fleas.' Lord knows Doyle's tiny as one."

Daddy snorted on his lemonade.

Briar grinned and took a gulp of her sweet tea, not wishing to be rude. The drink went down far smoother than the kind Grandpa Bob had made. Briar drained half the glass before hearing the screen door shut.

"All right, then, ol' buddy," Jesse Thomason's voice echoed from the other room. "What you got cooked up—"

He stopped in the doorway, his face paling as Briar's had at seeing all the food.

Doyle appeared beside him, grinning from ear to ear. "Hope you're hungry, pup." He clapped Jesse on the shoulder. "Seeing as my wife cooked all this heaven you asked for."

Briar had never seen Jesse Thomason so quiet.

After saying grace, they tucked into the meal.

Briar had two helpings of the mashed potatoes and noodles and loaded up on turkey. But for all she ate and watched the others eat, they never seemed able to put a dent in the food.

Time and again, she watched Doyle heap more onto Jesse's plate. A spoonful of green beans, or else another slice of ham— Jesse had no chance of cleaning his plate.

"I can't," Jesse said finally, warding Doyle off. "I can't eat no more. My belly's 'bout to pop."

Briar winced at the thought and saw Jesse's face pale when Doyle rose from the table.

"Shoot, boy." Doyle headed toward the countertop, returning a minute later with a new plate. On it, he'd heaped a slice of angel food cake, a piece of apple pie with a scoop of vanilla ice cream, and a chocolate chip cookie. Doyle grinned and switched the new plate out for Jesse's dirtied one. "You still got dessert."

Briar started to laugh, but Daddy pinched her shoulder again to hush her up.

Jesse pushed back from the table, sighing. "Doyle, I can't—"

"You best eat up now," said Grandpa Bob, his voice low and stern. "You done asked for it."

Briar rubbed her stomach, feeling it tight and full.

Jesse's face pained as he reached for the cookie first then put it to his mouth and nibbled off a piece.

Doyle hooted and sat back down next to Charlene. "Well, ain't this nice. Feels like old times don't it?"

"Food's better," said Grandpa Bob.

"Tastes the same to me." Doyle slapped Jesse on the arm. "Hey, Jess, won't you tell Bob over here how you plan to keep them rose-givers out this year."

Briar perked despite Jesse shaking his head.

He took another bite of the cookie.

"What's a matter, pup?" Doyle laughed. "You always got something to say."

"Won't matter." Grandpa Bob pour himself another glass of tea. "They'll get in anyway."

Briar heard her daddy's chair squeak. She looked on him and saw his cheeks tighten.

Doyle coughed down his laugh. "Ol' Jess plans on hiding out by the grave of Lainey Grace this year, Bob."

"Oh, really?"

"Yessir," said Doyle. "Gonna camp out by that there tree next to the burial space, ain't you, boy?"

Jesse swallowed down the rest of the cookie. "Why not?" He licked the corners of his mouth. "Figure if you two geezers wanna lay them roses this year, you'll have to come by me."

Daddy stirred next to Briar. "You ever sat out in the cemetery at night before, Jess?"

"'Course I have," said Jesse, though Briar thought his quavering tone suggested otherwise. He rubbed his forehead then picked up his fork and sliced off a bite of the angel food cake. "Why?"

Daddy nodded. "So you know how them headstones will play with your mind then."

"I don't," said Briar. "What do you mean, Daddy?"

"Yeah," said Jesse. "How do you mean?"

Daddy smirked and turned to Grandpa Bob. "You ever tell him about that time you and I waited for them rose-givers, Dad?"

Briar blinked. *Daddy tried to find them too?*

Grandpa Bob shook his head. "Only thing I told him is he won't find them, or stop them neither."

"Well, what happened?" Jesse asked.

"Ah, I guess it don't matter," said Daddy, slouching in his chair. "Seeing as you've been in there at night before. You know what to expect."

"Yeah, I know." said Jesse. He picked up his fork and pointed it at Doyle. "And just so you old timers know, I'm gonna have my gun on me too."

Grandpa Bob crossed his arms over his big belly. "That's asking for trouble."

"You's asking for trouble, if you find a way in after them gates are locked." Jesse let his fork clatter on the plate. "That's trespassing on private property after hours. And being head groundskeeper now, I'm within my rights to do whatever I got to—"

"You ain't got to do nothing," said Doyle.

"And you won't," said Grandpa Bob.

No. Briar folded her arms across her chest like Daddy and Grandpa Bob. *You won't. Trixie and his friends will get in anyway.*

Jesse rubbed his nose with the back of his hand. "Well, just so you know." He stared on Grandpa Bob. "I'll be in there waiting for you."

"You gonna be waiting a long time then."

Doyle stood from the table. "Yep. Just like old times." He patted his wife. "Charlene, you mind making our guest here a sack of food to take home. Seems his eyes were bigger than this stomach."

Charlene nodded and went about making Jesse another plate.

"I don't need nothing from you." Jesse backed his chair up, screeching it against the tile. "I know you done invited me here just to laugh at me with all this food."

"That what got you riled up all the time, Jess?" Grandpa Bob asked. "You think everyone's laughing at you?"

"My grandpa's trying to teach you something," said Briar. "Even I know that."

She felt another pinch in her shoulder from Daddy, a silent reprimand, but one that sent the message clear. Briar hushed up, though her whole body felt hot. She distracted herself listening to Charlene tying off the ends of a plastic bag with a plate full of food inside.

"Here you go." She handed the sack to Jesse. "Thank you for coming to our house."

Jesse's face reddened as he took the sack. "Thank you, ma'am," he muttered.

"I'll show you out," said Doyle.

"I'll see myself out." Jesse huffed and made a weak attempt at waving goodbye. "Night all."

Grandpa Bob alone replied. "Night, Jess."

Briar watched him leave and heard the front door shut, (quietly, to her surprise). The engine of Jesse's clunker fired a minute later and revved as he backed out of the drive, the tires kicking up gravel.

"Well," said Daddy. "We best get moving on for home too, Little Miss."

"But I wanna stay overnight with Grandpa," she said.

"Briar Ann," said Daddy in the tone that warned her not to argue. "Why don't you thank Mr. Doyle and Miss Charlene here for having us over tonight."

"Thank you for the food," said Briar.

Charlene nodded and Doyle winked at Briar as she rose from the table to go.

"Go give Grandpa a hug," said Daddy.

Briar obliged, trying to fit her arms around him. She couldn't. "Night, Grandpa," she said.

"Goodnight, Little Miss." He patted her back before she pulled away.

"Thanks again, Doyle," said Daddy, then nodding to Charlene. "Ma'am."

"Night, Russ."

Briar watched the two of them shake hands then she followed Daddy out of the house.

A hound dog lay on the porch, a collar around his neck and a leash attached to it. The dog lifted its head and looked on Briar, its fat tongue wagging and tail slapping against the wood floor.

Briar followed the leash and saw a rusted stake still tied to the other end.

Daddy leaned back inside the house. "Hey, Doyle," he called. "Your dog got loose."

Briar knelt and gave the hound a good rubbing behind the ears. "Hi, buddy. What's your name?"

But the dog only closed his eyes and panted.

"You're a good dog, ain't you?" Briar asked, scratching down his back and patting his side.

The hound rolled over and showed her his belly to rub.

Briar laughed and obliged him.

"Ain't got no dog," said Doyle, appearing in the door. He smirked at seeing Briar petting one though. "Well, lookie there. Told you ol' Shadow didn't have no fight in him, didn't I?"

Briar stopped petting the hound.

"Hmm," said Daddy. "This your neighbor's dog then?"

Doyle nodded. "Same one you heard barking earlier this evening."

Briar looked on the passive, thin hound and wondered how he ever made such a noise.

"Yessir." Doyle knelt and gave the hound a rougher petting than Briar had. "I think ol' Shadow likes it better over here. Hauls up his stakes and comes over 'bout every night. Neighbor still can't figure out how he's doing it." Doyle laughed. "Guess even an old dog still has his secret tricks, ain't you, boy?"

Briar swore the hound grinned at her before rolling over again to show Doyle his belly.

CHAPTER TEN

The Lesson

Briar closed the passenger door in Daddy's truck and buck-led up as he backed out of the drive onto State Road 39 and headed back in town.

"Well," he said. "What'd you think about tonight?"

Briar shrugged. "It was fun to see Jesse's face when he saw all that food."

"Yeah, that was something." Daddy chuckled. "But did you learn anything?"

"Charlene sure can cook," said Briar.

"Yes, ma'am, she can," said Daddy. "But I meant anything else. Were you keeping watch throughout tonight? Did you learn anything from that old dog and Jesse and Doyle too?"

"Like what?"

Daddy put his elbow on the door, resting his hand against the glass. "Things aren't always what they seem, Little Miss," he said. "Doyle taught me that way back when I worked at the cemetery and used to run my mouth off like Jesse. Thought Doyle wasn't nothing but some itty-bitty guy who couldn't hold his own against a young buck like me. Then I ended up flat on my back. Couple times, in fact."

Briar smiled at the thought of him tussling with Doyle. Then she thought of something else and wriggled in her chair.

"Daddy," she said.

"Yeah?"

"What'd you mean by the cemetery plays with your mind?" Briar asked.

"Oh, I probably shouldn't have said nothing. Don't need to give Jesse more ideas. Just trying to warn him is all." Daddy switched hands on the steering wheel, his jaw working back and forth. "Cemeteries can be funny at night," he said finally. "Makes you see things."

Briar reached for the thermostat, turning the heat up. "What kind of things?"

"Reflections, mostly," he said. "Them headstone act like mirrors. Even the tiniest ray of moonlight can make you think you seen a ghost when really it's just you moving on by."

Briar shuddered. "You go in there a lot?"

"When I was younger," he said. "Back when Dad had me convinced about them secret rose-givers, like he's got you fooled."

Briar thought of Trixie, but remembered her promise. *Daddy couldn't see him anyway.*

"No," he said. "The night I was talking about at dinner was when Dad and I hid inside the cemetery one fall, hoping to find the rose-givers. Only thing was, Jesse's uncle, Ted, had taken it on himself to have the police keep watch inside too." Daddy's tone dropped. "Only Ted didn't tell us about the police, and them cops didn't know we were inside either."

"That's stupid," said Briar. "Why not?"

Daddy cocked his head to the side. "Didn't trust us. Guess Ted thought it really was Dad and Doyle laying them roses. Wanted to catch them red-handed."

Briar's heart beat quicker as Daddy continued.

"So we were out there hiding. You know that big headstone down the way from Lainey Grace's, the Johnson spaces?"

"The long, black marble one?" Briar asked.

"No, that's their cousins," said Daddy. "I'm talking about the big red one a couple rows over."

Briar's forehead wrinkled as she tried to place it in her memory.

"Anyway," said Daddy. "Me and Dad were behind that. Didn't wanna get too close to Lainey Grace's grave, in case someone coming to lay them roses saw us and took off. We were out there, oh, I dunno"—Daddy blew a breath—"at least 'til two o'clock in the morning or so when Dad nudged me awake."

Briar sat up straighter. "What did you see?"

"Nothing, at first," said Daddy. "Just heard voices coming our way."

Briar thought of Trixie and grinned. "Did they rhyme a lot?"

"No," Daddy laughed. "They sounded like Howard Gozer and Mark Butcher."

"Who?"

"Cops," said Daddy. "Anyway, they were making their own rounds through the cemetery. We knew them pretty well and seen them in town all the time, so I thought it'd be fun to jump out and scare them."

Briar giggled. "You were gonna scare cops, Daddy?"

"Thought about it," he said. "Dad stopped me though. Good thing too. I didn't understand why at the time, but I do now, and it's because of that way the cemetery plays with people's minds at night."

"I don't understand."

"That's 'cause you've pretty much lived out there. Even if you went into the cemetery at night, you'd know there wasn't anything in there that weren't there during the day."

Briar kept back a grin, wondering if Daddy knew how wrong he was.

"But people are funny," he continued. "They let their imagination run with them, even when they know better."

"So what happened?" Briar asked.

"We just let them walk by," said Daddy. "They stopped by the cemetery the next morning and Dad told them how they walked right past us. Never even knew we were there."

Briar laughed. "That would've been funny if you had scared them."

"No, it wouldn't," said Daddy, his voice low. "Can you imagine what they'd have done if someone jumped out from behind a gravestone?"

"They just would've yelled at you is all," she said.

"Maybe," said Daddy. "Or maybe they would've drawn their guns and started shooting." Daddy shook his head. "That's what me, Dad, and Doyle was trying to tell Jesse tonight, but he wouldn't hear it. It's one thing to be scared. It's another to have a gun when you're in that kind of situation."

Briar glanced out the window as they came to the first stoplight in town, watching people enter the Denny's restaurant as other patrons left out the opposite door. Briar scratched her neck.

"Daddy," she said. "I thought Grandpa kept the only key to unlock the gates…"

He smirked, his dimples made visible by the security lights brightening the interior. "Caught that, did you?" Daddy eased on the gas when the traffic light turned green. "There used to be two keys. Dad had one and Jesse's uncle had the other. After that incident with us and the cops though, Dad said something to Mr. Coldwater about Ted letting them cops inside."

"So Mr. Coldwater took back the key?"

Daddy shrugged. "That's the story, according to Ted."

Briar slumped. *But if Ted kept that second key,* she thought. *That means he could get in too.* Briar reminded herself to warn Trixie about Jesse and the chance his uncle Ted might still have a key.

"Daddy?"

"Yeah, baby?"

"Why don't you believe in the rose-givers?" she asked, fiddling with the bottom of her shirt. "Why don't you believe Grandpa?"

"Briar…"

"I know you did once," she said. "Doyle told me."

"Well, he shouldn't have. They both need to quit telling you them stories and getting your hopes up."

"I like their stories," said Briar.

"That's fine," said Daddy. "Long as you know that's all they are."

But they're not. Briar kept back the thought, not wanting to stir Daddy up.

"I know it's hard to understand right now, baby, but I'm try-ing to save you pain," said Daddy. "Think I spent more days working in that cemetery than even you have. Came up with all sorts of traps and stuff trying to find them out. Never saw hide nor hair of them rose-givers though."

"But every year the roses come…"

"Yeah, they do," said Daddy. "But the older I got, the more I realized they didn't want me to see them doing it or find out why, whoever they are. There comes a time when you have to give up on that sort of thinking. Face facts."

"Grandpa and Doyle still believe in them," said Briar.

Daddy's grip squeaked on the steering wheel. "Baby, they just do that to get you going. They don't mean nothing bad by it, don't get me wrong, but them roses and wondering who brings them are just stories to pass the time."

Briar felt hot. "They're not just stories."

"They are, Little Miss," said Daddy. "If Doyle and Dad wanted to find out who really brought them in, they could. They know that cemetery better than anybody. I've been keep-ing my mouth shut, but you're getting old enough to start knowing better."

"Is that why you won't let me stay over with Grandpa any-more?" Briar asked as they turned into the driveway of their home.

Daddy put the truck in park but left the engine running as the stillness passed between them.

Briar grabbed for the door handle.

Daddy reached over to stop her. "Baby, I don't mean to keep you from spending time with Grandpa. He's just getting older now. Doesn't need to worry about whether you're getting into stuff you shouldn't be."

"What could I get into?" she asked. "He doesn't have anything in that apartment but those old westerns and them dahlia bulbs he dug up."

"Dahlia bulbs?" Daddy asked. "What he's doing with those?"

"Saving them 'til spring to plant again," she said. "He didn't want them to die and knew Jesse wouldn't take care of them."

Daddy frowned. "He shouldn't be going into the cemetery and digging those up. That's not his job anymore. Not his place."

"Well, what else is he supposed to do?" she asked. "Every time I go over, he's just sitting in his chair, watching westerns, alone in the dark."

Daddy sat back.

Briar nodded. "That's why I wanted to stay over with him tonight."

"I know, baby, but that's not what Grandpa needs right now."

"How do you know?" she asked. "I don't ever see you over there."

Daddy flushed. "Just 'cause you don't see me, don't mean I ain't stopped by or talked with Grandpa on the phone," he said. "He's up a lot at night nowadays. And you don't need to be over there to see that or worry about him being up at all hours."

Briar felt her stomach tighten. "Is he sick or something?"

"No, baby," said Daddy, putting his arm around her. "He's just getting old."

Briar shrugged away from him. "He's not that old," she said. "Why do you and Grandpa keep saying that?"

"Because it's truth, baby," he said. "It ain't easy to hear, but it hurts less than lies."

Briar glanced out the truck window, allowing the silence return between them.

"Tell you what," said Daddy. "Why don't you and I go visit Grandpa tomorrow together. That work for you?"

Briar turned. "You mean it?"

"I do," he said. "Soon as I get home from work, we'll head over. Just make sure you don't stay out too late playing with Trixie." Daddy reached for the door handle. "Say…when are we gonna meet her by the way?"

"Trixie's a *he*, Daddy," she said.

"Oh…" He grimaced. "Well, even more reason to bring him by then."

Weeds

"Do you see him, Trixie?" Briar hissed.

"Aye, he goes to the barn, that smug little man. Quick, now's the time! Let's be off with your plan!"

Briar waited until Jesse entered the barn. Then she kicked off the pavement and gave the pedals a whirl, speeding her through the main cemetery archway. She veered left and headed for the biggest of the dinner-plate dahlia flowerbeds in the cemetery that Grandpa Bob had planted near the Wade family burial spaces and plot.

Trixie glanced all around. "Shouldn't be in here. We shouldn't have came. And if we get caught, it's Briar I'll blame."

"Oh, be quiet," said Briar, moving the gardening shovel that shared the tin bucket space he rode in. "We won't be long. It's not like you had to come."

She parked her bicycle against a hickory tree. Fetching her gardening trowel and pruning shears from the tin bucket wired to her handlebars, (and after allowing Trixie to run up her arm), Briar ran for the flowerbed with him on her shoulder.

"Grandpa Bob is going to love this surprise," she said. "He couldn't save as many dahlias as he wanted on account of he's too slow to get in and out of the cemetery without Jesse knowing."

Briar slipped off her backpack. Unzipping the side, she took out the black plastic flowerpot she had rescued from the trash.

"But we'll get him more," she said.

Briar picked up her gardening trowel and plunged its shovel tip into the dirt, loosening up the hardened earth. Then she jerked on the tuber stem to yank out the dahlia bulbs and set them aside for pruning.

Trixie climbed down her arm and inspected her dig-site. "Ah, look at ye go, ye wee mole rat. Tell Trixie now, where'd ye learn to do that?"

"Grandpa Bob showed me," she said. "He showed me lots of stuff like this."

Trixie nodded, then danced away as Briar continued with the flowerbed.

Briar made quick work of the dahlia bed and took out her pruning shears, snipping down to the dirt-dusted bulb bases.

"Pretty neat, huh?" Briar asked, holding up the dahlia bulb.

Trixie said nothing in reply.

"Trixie?" Briar turned, but the leprechaun was nowhere to be found. "Where'd you go?"

A shadow hovered over her.

"Just what you think you're doing?" Jesse Thomason asked her.

Briar gulped. "Uh, helping?"

"Trespassing, more like," said Jesse, taking her by the arm and hauling Briar to her feet. "Ain't I told you to stay out?"

"Yeah, but—"

"But nothing," he said. "You ain't got no right to come in here and dig up these flowers. These belong to the cemetery."

"My grandpa planted these, so I got all the rights I need," said Briar. "'Sides, the frost wiped them out already and you'll lose them for good if you don't dig up these bulbs before a deep freeze hits."

"Well, ain't you just Miss Smarty-Pants," said Jesse. "That geezer tell you to come in here and do his dirty work for him?"

"Grandpa Bob didn't send me," said Briar. "I wanted to get these to surprise him."

"Oh, it's gonna be a surprise, I reckon." He motioned toward her bicycle. "Let's go."

"What do you mean?" she asked.

"You know what I mean," he said. "We gonna get your bike and head to the groundskeeper office. Gotta call your daddy to come get you."

"No!" Briar tried to shrug away.

Jesse clamped harder. "I done warned you already too many times, and you ain't listened."

"But—"

"You rather I call the police instead?"

Briar slumped.

"That's what I thought," said Jesse. "Come on now."

Jesse led Briar to her bicycle and allowed her to put the tools back inside. He didn't loosen his grip on her one bit as he took hold of the steering wheel with his other hand and walked both she and bicycle up the paved drive.

"Yeah," he said. "I'll bet y'all had a real good laugh after I left Doyle's shack last night, didn't you?"

Briar kept her mouth shut.

"Yep," said Jesse. "That's what I thought. Everyone poking fun at ol' Jess. Well, it's my turn today, Sister Sue. Gonna be real funny when your daddy comes to pick you up for sneaking in here again."

Briar bit her tongue to keep from firing back at him. She didn't break her silence until they reached the main gate.

Daddy's truck was parked outside the cemetery office, half in the lawn.

Jesse spit. "He's gonna tear up my yard parking like that."

Briar felt the hairs on the back of her neck raise. *Daddy knows better.*

The groundskeeper office door opened and Momma stepped out with Doyle. Her face was red and she fanned herself at seeing Briar.

"Jess," said Doyle. "Turn her loose."

"Uh uh," said Jesse. "Caught me a trespasser. Might be I need to file a—"

"Bob's in the hospital," said Doyle.

Jesse's grip loosened. "What?"

Briar broke free of him and ran for Momma. "Why do you have Daddy's truck?"

"He's already at the hospital and wanted me to come find you," she said. "I been looking everywhere for you."

Briar trembled. "What's wrong, Momma?"

"I don't know, baby," she said. "But we got to hurry. Doyle—"

"Yes, ma'am?" the Kentuckian stepped forward, removing his hat.

"Will you load up her bicycle for us?"

Jesse wheeled it on ahead. "I'll do it."

Briar sneered as he passed her, though she couldn't deny he was better suited to the task then Doyle. Jesse lifted the bicycle with one hand up and over the truck side, laying it gently in the plastic bed.

"Come on, Briar Ann," said Momma.

Briar ran to the truck and flung open the door.

"You give Bob our best now, Little Miss," said Doyle. "You hear?"

"Yessir, I will," she said, slamming the door as Momma got in on the other side.

Momma backed the truck out in a hurry, and Briar was just sure she had indeed torn up a bit of the lawn in doing so. The truck picked up speed as they headed into town.

"Momma, what happened to Grandpa?" Briar asked.

"They think it's his heart," she said. "I don't know much more than that. Your daddy got the call at work, then swung by the house to pick me up on the way to the hospital."

"Well, have you seen him?" Briar asked. "Did you see Grandpa?"

"No, baby," she said. "Your daddy's with him though. He talked with the doctors and said I best find you. Figured you'd wanna see Grandpa, if the nurses will let you."

They ain't gonna stop me, Briar thought.

Briar sat back hard against her seat when Momma sped through town faster than usual and ran a few yellow lights.

They had to pass by Grandpa's apartment complex on the way to the hospital. Briar saw his navy truck still parked outside.

Briar leaned her head against the passenger side window, watching the truck fade in the rearview after Momma passed by. *How can he not be there if his truck is?*

Momma banked a hard right into the hospital parking lot, forcing Briar to brace against the dash to not smack against the glass. They both hopped out of the truck no sooner than it was in park and headed for the hospital entrance.

The automatic doors whooshed open, blasting Briar in the face with cold air. Her nose wrinkled at the deep smell of sterile cleaning supplies, reminding her of the old folk's home they had put Grandma in before she died.

Briar followed her mother to the registration desk, her gaze wandering over the collection of people in the waiting room. Babies crying, a man with his leg in a cast and crutches at his side, a mom yelling at three kids to hush up.

"Room 412?" Momma said. "Okay, thank you. Come along, Briar Ann."

She trailed after Momma to the elevators and pressed the button to call it. It dinged a second later, behind them, and Briar turned to watch the silver doors slide open.

Others crowded into the elevator with them, one of them a little boy no older than five or six. His daddy helped him press the 3rd floor button.

"Four, please," said Momma.

The little boy obliged by pressing all the buttons.

Briar wondered if the boy had a sick grandpa too. But when he got off with his daddy at the third floor, she read the labor and delivery sign posted just outside near the ceiling.

The elevator door closed and Briar slumped against the corner.

"Don't slouch, Briar Ann." Momma tugged under her arm.

"Why not?" Briar asked. "There ain't no one in here but us."

Momma glanced up to the camera in the corner. "A lady needs mind her manners all the time."

"I ain't no lady yet," Briar muttered as she straightened.

She felt the thrumming beneath the floor stop.

The doors opened again a second later.

Briar followed Momma out and around the corner.

There was a waiting room at the end of the hall with a TV playing the local news. Briar noticed a couple of her uncles and aunts seated behind the glass wall, talking among themselves.

Momma strode to join them, but didn't check to see if Briar followed.

I don't wanna wait in there, Briar thought. She looked at the signs dangling from the ceiling and, glancing back to ensure Momma wasn't watching, Briar headed down the hall toward room 412.

She hurried past the nursing station when they weren't looking and slunk to the end of the corridor, her footsteps echoing off the linoleum flooring. Briar counted the numbers of each door and felt a rising flutter in her stomach as she reached the end of the hall. She paused in front of the door to room 412, finding it half-shut and mostly dark inside.

Briar nudged it open, peeking around the edge.

The first thing she saw was Daddy.

Seated in a cheap, maroon plastic chair at the foot of the bed, Daddy had bent over, both elbows resting on his knees, hands propping up his head and shielding his face.

"D-Daddy," said Briar, stepping into the room.

He glanced up, his eyes red-stained. "Briar?" Daddy asked, standing. "How'd you get here, baby?"

"Momma brought me," she said, her gaze hovering on the bed and the white, fuzzy blankets that covered someone's feet. A pale light shone from around that corner, spotlighting the bed.

Grandpa, she thought. *Grandpa's in that bed.*

Briar felt her own feet rooted to the floor. "Daddy, what's wrong with Grandpa?"

Daddy licked his lips. "Well, honey—"

"Getting old, Little Miss," Grandpa Bob's throaty voice croaked from beyond the wall. "Just getting old."

Daddy waved her step closer. "Come here, baby."

Briar shook her head and she glanced toward the hall when Daddy walked over to her.

"Your grandpa wants to see you, Little Miss," he whispered. "Now, you come on."

With Daddy's guiding hand on her back, Briar stepped hesitantly onward, wincing the more she saw of Grandpa Bob.

Propped up by the mechanical bed, the fluorescent light shone behind his head. His hair was uncombed, black and greasy, per usual, and his tinted glasses lay on the bedside table next to a pink plastic jug and an uneaten food tray.

For the time in her memory, Briar thought she saw his face plain.

Crow's feet wrinkles adorned the corners of Grandpa Bob's brown eyes and day-old black whiskers shadowed his cheeks that Briar had only ever seen clean-shaven.

"That you, Little Miss?" he asked, squinting.

Briar stood transfixed by all the tubes and wires. They hung from a metal pole and attached to Grandpa Bob, plugging his nose and running into his arms. Still others ran into unseen places beneath the blankets.

Weeds, Briar thought of the wired mess ensnaring Grandpa Bob. *They look like weeds.*

Her fingers stirred with the urge to pluck the weeds, just as he taught her to help flowers bloom and grow.

Grandpa Bob lifted his left hand that had a white bracelet wrapped around his wrist and still another IV running into his veins. "This looks like a bad deal, don't it?" he asked her, his voice weak, despite his grin.

Briar nodded. "Grandpa, what happened?"

"Oh, don't think I got much gas left in the tank, Little Miss." Grandpa Bob reached for the pink jug on his bedside table, his face contorted in pain.

"I'll get it," said Daddy.

Briar backed away from the bed as he walked around to pour some more ice water. Then he leaned over and put the straw to Grandpa Bob's mouth.

Grandpa Bob sipped on it, then coughed a bit and licked his lips. "Thank you," he said, his eyes flitting to Briar. "Ain't you gonna come over, Little Miss?"

Briar shambled to the bed.

"There," said Grandpa Bob, smiling. "Now I can see you with these old peepers. Say, Russ…"

"Yeah, Dad?"

"Won't you gimme a minute with Little Miss here," said Grandpa Bob.

Briar glanced to Daddy.

"You all right?" he asked.

"She'll be okay," said Grandpa Bob. "Just nervous a bit, ain't you?"

Briar nodded.

"Go on, Russ," said Grandpa Bob. "We'll be fine 'til you get back. Why don't you bring me a soda."

"Dad, you're not—"

"I know," he said. "But what're them nurses gonna do? Kick me out? Bring me back a Coca-Cola, son."

Briar fought back a grin as Daddy shook his head and stepped out of the room.

"Well now," said Grandpa Bob. "Just you and me again, Little Miss. Just like old times."

Briar chewed on her bottom lip as she sat at his side. "What happened to you, Grandpa?"

"Heart attack, they think," he said. "I whooped Doyle in a game of cards 'fore driving home last night. Must've been too much excitement for my old ticker."

Briar's bottom lip quivered.

"Aw," he said, taking hold of her hand. "What's wrong with you now?"

"Are you..." she sniffed. "Are you dying, Grandpa?"

"Oh, I reckon so," he said. "Have been for a while now."

Briar's eyes welled up. "W-why?"

"Figure I don't wanna give your grandma too much time to tell stories on me," he said. "She might just rat me out of them angels writing my name in the good book."

Briar fought back a grin. "Grandma wouldn't do that."

His bushy eyebrows raised. "She might," he said. "Might be

she found some good looking angel up there to run around with while I've been stuck down here."

"Maybe..." Briar wiped her eyes. "Maybe you could find someone down here then."

"Oh, I dunno if I wanna go through that circus again." He smirked, revealing the Wade dimples. "'Sides, might be them angels will tell me who lays them roses on the grave of Lainey Grace. Shoot, I might even find her up there myself."

"I can tell you, Grandpa," Briar sputtered the words. "I can tell you who lays them roses."

"Oh, yeah?"

Briar nodded. "It's Trixie and his friends." The words spilled out. "He's a leprechaun that got himself caught in one of Doyle's traps last year. I got me a second wish coming up."

"Second one, huh?" asked Grandpa Bob. "What you think you might use it on?"

"I dunno," she said. "I only get one each year, but Trixie says I gotta wait until the last leaf of summer falls before I can use it."

Grandpa Bob pointed to the window. "You best be thinking on it then. Don't guess them leaves'll last much longer."

"M-Maybe Trixie can make you better, Grandpa." Briar swallowed hard. "I could wish for you to get better or—"

"Don't know as I'd let you," he said. "Wishes is a special thing. Don't need to go wasting one on an old man like me. 'Sides, if he's a real leprechaun, might be you should have him lead you to a big pot of gold."

"I don't care about no gold," said Briar.

"Then you're smarter than you know," said Grandpa Bob.

"Wouldn't trust a leprechaun to give me a pot of gold anyhow. He'd find a way to trick me and take it back, no doubt."

Briar sniffled even as her face broke into a wide grin. "He tricked me last year into using a wish." She rubbed her nose. "I wanted to unlock the gates and see all the rose-givers, but Trixie wouldn't grant it then on account of I didn't say when."

"See?" Grandpa Bob chuckled and coughed. "Gotta watch them leprechauns. Wily devils." He coughed again. "They used to steal..." Grandpa Bob rubbed his chest. "Your grandma's... radishes—"

He coughed, deep and loud, and it kept on longer than any other fit Briar had seen him have.

"Grandpa—" Briar stood from the bed, her pulse racing at his continued hacking. "*Grandpa!*"

Briar started for the door.

"I'm all right," Grandpa Bob said, breathing hard and raspy. He coughed again, but gained control of it quicker. "I'm all right."

Briar heard footsteps running down the hall.

Daddy and a nurse came around the corner.

"You okay, Bob?" the nurse asked, striding around the bed and checking the monitor hooked up to him.

"I'm fine," he said. "Just got a little carried away."

"All the same," said the nurse. "I think it best you get some rest now."

Grandpa Bob smiled. "Lemme say bye to my Little Miss first."

Briar felt the nurse's gaze fall on her.

"Be quick then," said the nurse before leaving the room.

Briar approached the bed and saw Grandpa Bob opening his

big paw of a hand to her. She took it and felt fingers the size of sausages squeeze her. Briar's vision blurred.

"Why, your hands got dirt on them, Little Miss," he said. "What you been doing?"

"Digging," she said, her voice breaking with all the memories of times she'd spent next to him with their hands in the dirt. "I went out to the cemetery today and dug up some more of them dahlias you talked about."

"Oh-ho," said Grandpa Bob. "Dahlias, huh?"

"Yessir," she said, not wanting to tell him that she forgot them when Jesse had grabbed her. "I thought you'd wanna put them in that apple crate of yours. Thought maybe we'd plant them together in the spring."

"Well, that'd be nice wouldn't it?" he asked.

"It *will* be," said Briar.

Grandpa Bob reached his other arm across his chest to pat her hand. "Come here, now."

Briar leaned on the bed and felt his unshaved cheeks scratch hers. She sniffed back her tears and caught a whiff of his minty deodorant.

Then the dam broke.

"Grandpa," she shuddered. "Don't die...please."

"Oh, we all got to someday," said Grandpa Bob. "Dying's a part of life. Even them dahlias got to wither come the fall."

"But they come back in the spring," she said.

"Might be I'll find me a way back too." Grandpa Bob held her closer. "I love you, Little Miss," he whispered, patting her back. "Love you more every day. Ain't nothing can change that. Not even dying, you hear?"

"Grandpa…"

"You get on, now," he said. "Go find that leprechaun friend of yours and tell him he best pay up on that wish you made. If not, I'll come looking for him."

Briar fought to stay in his grip when she felt Daddy tug on her shirt.

"Come on, Briar Ann," he said. "Grandpa needs his rest."

"I don't wanna leave. I wanna stay with Grandpa."

Daddy's face flushed. "Baby—"

"I wanted to stay with him last night and you didn't let me!" Briar yelled. "If you had let me stay, he wouldn't be here. I could've helped."

Daddy's lip quivered. "Briar—"

"No," she said.

"Briar Ann," Grandpa Bob's stern voice called her down. "You listen to your Daddy now."

"Why?" she asked through her tears. "He don't listen to me or you, Grandpa. I told him you needed a job, so you wouldn't be so sad. Maybe if he had went up and talked to Mr. Coldwater last year—"

"That ain't fair, now," said Grandpa Bob. "Your daddy ain't got nothing to do with me losing that job. You let this go, you hear?"

Briar ran out of the room, Daddy's holler and his footsteps behind her feeding the flames coursing through her veins. All the way down the hall, Briar kept running, not stopping until Daddy caught her near the elevator.

Briar turned and fell into his arms, sobbing. "Daddy…"

"I know, baby." He palmed the back of her head, holding her against his shoulder. "I know."

~CHAPTER TWELVE~

Cats & Dogs

"Momma, why couldn't I stay with Daddy and Grandpa?"

"Baby," said Momma. "Hospitals aren't a place kids ought be. Your daddy needs to focus on Grandpa right now."

"But I could help—"

"Briar, we've been over this."

Briar glared out the window and didn't say another word all the way home. *I can still help.*

An idea of *how* she might help came when they turned in the drive. "Momma, can we get my bicycle out of the back?"

"Honey, you don't need to be out riding your bicycle right now," said Momma. "If Daddy calls—"

"Please," said Briar.

"I appreciate you saying please," said Momma, parking the truck and turning off the engine. "But we're gonna stay at home for now."

Briar got out of the truck and slammed the door.

"*Briar Ann!*" said Momma.

"The door slipped out of my hand," she said.

"Uh huh." Momma placed her hand on her hip. "My hand is gonna slip if you don't cool your attitude, Little Miss."

Briar put her head down and leaned against the truck. "Sorry," she mumbled.

"What was that?"

"Sorry," said Briar.

"That's better." Momma went inside the house.

Briar waited a moment then ran to the back of the truck. Struggling to lower the tailgate without letting it slam, she climbed inside and dragged her bicycle to the edge. Then she tipped it over the side where it clattered on the cement.

Briar glimpsed Momma in the kitchen window, moving toward the main door of their house. She jumped from the truck bed and picked up her bicycle, swinging her leg over the side. Then she kicked hard, pedaling away from her house.

"Briar Ann!" Momma called behind her, the clacking of her heels running up the drive after her. "Where you going?"

Briar didn't answer. Tears stung her cheeks and hate fueled her muscles in riding out of town toward the cemetery.

The tin bucket rattled against the handlebars with all the speed she gathered. For a moment, Briar wondered what Trixie would say of such speed. Then she kicked the thought away, furious at him too for not being around to grant her a second wish.

She wheeled into the cemetery drive toward the main gate, never slowing as she rode past the groundskeeper office. Out of the corner of her eye, she caught sight of Jesse with his feet up on the desk that Grandpa Bob used to occupy.

Briar screamed and pedaled harder, uncaring that she disturbed the cemetery silence today. Nor did she hold her breath when passing under the arch. She followed the curve right, the wind buzzing in her ears.

On and on through the cemetery she rode, each spin of her pedals bringing her closer to the private drive of Mr. Coldwater. She took in the approaching sight of the stone archway and found the gargoyles held no power over her.

She flew under their stares and drove up the private drive, snaking a path onward through the ashes and elms lining either side.

Briar thought the trees resembled another natured wall, their fat–bottomed trunks close enough to touch and their nearly naked branches like bony fingers arching over her, blotting out the sun the further in she rode.

She felt the gazes of secret creatures hidden in their hollows as she kept on toward the Coldwater mansion, finding the air chillier, the darkened canopy blanketing.

The drive emptied in a roundabout with a long–empty fountain at its center. Red, orange, and yellow leaves filled its pool, the faces of the mermaid and selkie statues at its center chipped and stained.

Briar rode a circle around the fountain to slow her speed then walked her legs beside the bicycle and paced it. She glared at the mermaid statues, not trusting their icy stares or even the selkies' puppy-dog eyes.

The Coldwater's brick mansion loomed over her, its windows darkened by shades.

Briar dragged her feet to stop. Her heart wavered upon

abandoning the bicycle to clatter against the fountain. She glanced up at the second-floor windows, swearing she saw the shades move.

"Hey!" Briar called out.

The shades didn't move again.

Briar thought of Grandpa Bob and strode toward the doublewide oak doors.

Golden knockers crafted into lion faces hung at the center of each entry with silver rings in their mouths.

Briar reached for one of the rings and clapped it hard against the door.

The domed patio echoed the clapping to thunder over her and Briar winced, covering her ears.

Still, no one came.

Briar's nostrils flared. "Hey!"

Again, she clapped the doorknockers.

Again, no one came to answer.

Briar kicked the door. She stomped back to the fountain and glared up at the second story window.

"You put my grandpa in the hospital!" she yelled. "He loved that cemetery more than anything and now he's dying on account of you!"

The door creaked open.

Briar's shoulders raised at the sound. She turned back as an orange tomcat ran out of the house, straight for her. But rather than hiss and scratch, as she feared it might do, the cat only meowed and threaded through her legs.

Briar knelt to pet it, swearing the tomcat was one of those she'd seen out near the cemetery equipment barn. She loved on his face and trained her hand over the cat's arched back as she petted across it, each pet soothing the anger in her.

The tomcat closed his big brown eyes, purring louder.

"Thomas," said a voice from the door. "Thomas, come back—oh."

Briar glanced up from the cat.

A tiny elderly woman stood in the door, her brilliant white-blonde hair curled and her blue eyes sparkling.

"Why, hello, dear," she said, clasping her hands together and smiling.

Briar swore the woman's voice reminded her of Trixie's in a way, light and airy, slightly accented. Warmth spread through Briar. "Hello."

"Was that you at the door, just now, dearie?" asked the old woman.

"Yes, ma'am."

"Ah," she clapped. "Come for a bit of tea and biscuits, have we?"

Briar glanced back at her bicycle. "N-no, I came t-to…"

"Oh, but you must!" The old woman bustled out the door and threaded her arm around Briar's and led her to the mansion. "We never have company to speak of, and me shut up in here with that miser too."

The cat mewed.

"Come along then, Thomas," said the old woman. "Won't do to stay out here and have this darling girl catch her death of cold now, will it?"

The cat meowed louder, but the old woman wouldn't stop.

"As you please then," she said over her shoulder, not bothered.

"We're going inside where it's nice and warm. And we're going to have ourselves a wee little chat—"

The cat growled.

"*Thomas.*" The old woman turned and shook her finger at him. "That's quite enough of that, thank you very much. We'll not be listening to you any longer if you're going to act so sour. Run along now. Shoo!"

Briar watched as Thomas skittered across the yard and dashed back inside the mansion.

The old woman *tsk*ed. "Such a finicky creature, that Thomas. You like cats then too, dear?"

"Y-yes, ma'am," said Briar.

The old woman beamed. "Me muther oft said we women were like cats and men like dogs. I've found us quite the opposite. Cats only like you when they need, then off they go to their own world again and them at the center of it. Quite like men, in my opinion."

Briar snorted.

The old woman tittered. "But dogs are good, loyal creatures." She patted Briar's hand and led her toward the house. "Show a wee bit of kindness and love, and they'll stay by your side through the darkest of times. We women are like dogs, the drooling aside, of course." Her nose wrinkled. "Nasty habit, that. Drooling."

Briar hesitated when they reached the stoop.

"Why, what's wrong, dearie?"

"I-I don't—"

"Come inside. Have a biscuit or three," said the old woman. "That's why you came isn't it?"

"No, ma'am," said Briar. "I came to see M-Mr. Coldwater."

"That old goat?" She waved a hand. "You'd have been out here ages if waiting for him to answer the door. Hardly leaves his study, that one."

Briar glanced back to the fountain.

An autumn wind swept across the drive, swirling a whirl-wind of leaves in its wake.

Briar shivered. "I best get home—"

"You'll do nothing of the sort, dear," she said. "As it happens, Eamon will be soon to take his tea for the day too."

"Wh-who is Eamon?" Briar asked, thinking it sounded an awfully lot like the *amen* the preacher man said when ending his prayers.

"Why, Mr. Coldwater, dear," she said, her eyes twinkling as she grinned. "And I'm Mrs. Coldwater."

"You're his wife?" Briar asked.

"I am," said Mrs. Coldwater. "But don't you be holding that against me now, mind you. I was just a wee lass when Eamon tricked me into settling down with him, the rascally schemer. Fooled me proper, he did. Thought I had my shining prince, then he turned into an old, warty toad."

Briar grinned.

"You'll have some tea, then?" asked Mrs. Coldwater.

Briar glanced to the open door, wondering what lay beyond. She looked back to Mrs. Coldwater and felt the warm feeling spread within her. "Yes, ma'am," said Briar.

"Oh, lovely," Mrs. Coldwater clapped and dabbed her eye. "It's been far too long since we've had such a young spirit in this home. And—oh, where are my manners, dear. What did you say your name was?"

"Briar, ma'am. Briar Ann Wade."

Mrs. Coldwater touched her long, thin fingers under Briar's chin. "Ah, of course, it is. Beautiful and strong, aren't you?"

"I-I think so," said Briar.

"Aye, but you are," said Mrs. Coldwater. "And don't never let anyone tell you otherwise. Now, come. Time to fetch Eamon for his tea."

Briar gasped as she stepped across the threshold into the Coldwater mansion.

A silver chandelier hung above her, with dried wax clinging to the sides of a hundred candles. A set of twin marble stairwells stood before her, ascending to a landing then breaking off to stretch wide onto the second floor.

Briar thought the stairs looked as though they formed a giant X, bathed in the light of a wall of windowpanes that ran from floor to the third floor ceiling. Wrought iron banisters lined the steps, their metal tendrils swooping like the ivy that shrouded the cemetery's wall.

"Wh-why do you have two staircases?" Briar asked.

"Why, one for going up and the other for coming down," said Mrs. Coldwater in such a way that Briar wondered if the old woman had ever considered only a single stairwell.

A clock sounded from somewhere inside the home, its ominous ring striking three times.

"Oh dear," said Mrs. Coldwater, leading Briar toward the right stairwell. "We'll be late if we don't hurry."

Briar shrunk at she and Mrs. Coldwater's echoed footfalls as they hurried up the first series of marble steps and then onto the next. Briar's head swiveled as she took in the sights surrounding her.

Candelabras hung off the sides of mahogany-paneled walls, their candles gone and the holsters dusty. White sheets had been draped over what Briar assumed were paintings.

Mrs. Coldwater led her up the hall toward the last room on the left.

Briar shuddered when the wind howled outside the window.

"Don't be afraid, dear," said Mrs. Coldwater. "He's naught but a curmudgeon. He whines a wee bit like Thomas, but he'll heed me all the same, don't you worry."

Mrs. Coldwater nudged open the door and tugged Briar to follow her inside.

Briar edged around the door. At the first sight of Mr. Coldwater's study, her hand flew to cover her mouth. "Oh!"

Books lined shelves throughout the room, the golden letters on the tomes glittering in the firelight. A black marbled hearth lay at the far end of the room, its logs popping and crackling, sputtering orange sparks up into the chimney.

Two suits of armor bookended the hearth. A broadsword with a green plaid cloth wrapped around its hilt hung above the mantle, just beneath a coat of arms featuring three white fish with a bright crimson backdrop.

Mrs. Coldwater left Briar's side and approached the sprawling oak desk at the center of the room, its polished top covered with scattered parchment and half-empty glasses of water and wine. Balls of wadded up parchment lined the floor near an overflowing wastebasket.

Briar turned her head sideways to read the only bit legible from a distance, a flowing title written in an elegant cursive hand: *The Ainslian Tales.*

She sighed and righted herself to stare at the stuffed raven atop the desk, its wings poised aloft, frozen in time. Briar gazed around the room and found more oddities still: a plumed peacock feather, a skull of a creature with large fangs, and a geode the size of a watermelon.

"Eamon, dear."

Mrs. Coldwater's voice drew Briar's attention back to the desk.

The leather chair behind the desk turned. A wisp of a man sat in it, his face sallow and gaunt, and Briar wondered if he had been struck by lightning on account of what little hair remaining him shot to all sides in silver and black tufts.

He leaned in the chair, looking past his wife, his gaze falling on Briar.

"Who are you?" the man asked in a haggard voice.

"Uh…"

"You do not recall?" he asked.

Mrs. Coldwater tapped him on the shoulder. "That's rather rude of you," she said to her husband. "This girl's our guest, come for tea and biscuits."

"And where is our loyal manservant?" Mr. Coldwater asked, glancing to a chestnut clock in the corner. "Late, as usual."

"He'll be in shortly, dear," said Mrs. Coldwater. "He's not as young as he once was."

"Neither are you," he said.

Briar chuckled.

Mr. Coldwater's gaze fell on her again and she hushed up.

"At least she has a sense of humor," he said, struggling to rise from his chair, waving off his wife when she stepped near to help.

Mr. Coldwater grabbed up a silver cane, its handle sculpted into a dragon's head. He arched and leaned hard on it as he walked around the desk toward the leather sofas and chairs surrounding a small, round table.

"A guest, eh?" he asked. "What brings you here, little girl? Selling cookies?"

"No, sir," said Briar.

"Shame," he said. "I could do with some of the mint chocolate. Better than the dried, crumbly things Dmitri serves. Ah!" Mr. Coldwater pointed his cane toward the door. "Speak of the devil."

Briar turned as a tall, broad-shouldered, lean man waltzed into the room with a silver tray. Clean-shaven and dressed in a royal blue suit and tie, his receding black hair was slicked back.

Briar thought he looked like a vampire.

"Good evening, miss," Dmitri said to Briar.

"Hello."

"Ah, Dmitri," said Mrs. Coldwater. "You never miss a thing, do you? Thank you, dear, for bringing us a third teacup and plate. How did you know?"

"A gentleman never tells his secrets, madam." Dmitri said as he poured tea in all three cups. Then he waved his hand over the tea tray. "Enjoy."

Briar frowned when Dmitri smiled at her, as she noticed he had no fangs. But when he left the room, his feet moved so quickly she began to second-guess her deduction, swearing he glided.

Dmitri bowed out of the room and swung the door closed.

"So," said Mr. Coldwater, snapping off a bit of the cookie, staring at Briar. "Who are you?"

"Oh, do leave her alone for a moment," said Mrs. Coldwater. "At least allow the poor girl to sit down first."

Mr. Coldwater glowered and ate the rest of his hardened cookie, munching it slowly.

"Come along, dear." Mrs. Coldwater patted the sofa cushion next to her. "Sit beside me."

Briar shifted on her heels, then obliged.

Mrs. Coldwater beamed at her husband. "Isn't this nice?"

"I don't suppose so," said Mr. Coldwater, reaching for his tea. "It seems you've invited a vagrant into our home."

"I ain't no vagrant," said Briar.

"*Aren't*," he said. "And I hardly expect you know what a vagrant is, child."

"*Eamon!*" Mrs. Coldwater scolded.

Briar crossed her arms. "I do so know what it means. It's kinda like an orphan, like in *Oliver Twist*."

Mr. Coldwater set his tea back upon the tray. "You've read Dickens?"

"Yessir," said Briar. "And lots of other books too. Probably even some you ain't got in this room."

Mrs. Coldwater choked on her tea.

Mr. Coldwater leered at Briar. "A school assignment, no doubt."

"No, sir," said Briar. "I like to read."

Mr. Coldwater leaned forward. "*Who are you?*"

"I'm Briar Ann Wade," she said.

His lips pursed at her answer and his cleft chin lifted so that he might better look down his sharp, pointed nose. "Never heard of you."

"Well, I know who you are," she said. "You're Mr. Coldwater."

"Am I?" he asked, his eyes squinting. "Perhaps this foolish old woman lied to you. What if I were merely another manservant of Mr. Coldwater's, playing at his evil bidding?"

"No," said Briar. "I know that man. You ain't that mean Mr. Ted who runs your businesses."

Mr. Coldwater chuckled. "Perhaps I am worse."

"You are," said Briar, her body shaking as her answer hushed him up. "My grandpa worked in your cemetery since before my daddy was born. He done a good job all these years and you let your man Ted fire him on account of them rose–givers laying—"

"Rose-givers?" Mrs. Coldwater asked.

"Yes, ma'am," said Briar. "Them ones who bring in the roses every fall and lay them on the grave of Lainey Grace."

Mrs. Coldwater looked to her husband. "What is she talking about, Eamon?"

Mr. Coldwater took up his tea again, slurping it.

"Don't you read the newspaper?" Briar asked. "Or talk to people in town?"

"No," said Mrs. Coldwater. "We've not taken it in years and what few friends we once had in town have long since moved on."

"Well, they ain't stopped bringing roses," said Briar. "Been doing it ever since I know." She nodded at Mr. Coldwater. "And they're gonna keep doing it too. Every year, when the last leaf of summer falls, you'll see."

"Who, dear?" asked Mrs. Coldwater. "Who brings the roses?"

Briar hesitated. "I only know one of them."

"Well, then can you tell us, dear?" Mrs. Coldwater asked. "You can trust us."

"It ain't about trusting you or no," said Briar. "I promised him I wouldn't."

Mr. Coldwater stroked his cheeks with long, bony fingers. "Did Bob send you here? Is he ready to confess?"

"No, sir," she said. "He's in the hospital. No one sent me."

"Then why have you come?" he asked.

"'Cause you fired my grandpa," said Briar. "And just 'cause them rose-givers came in again to lay their roses on the grave of Lainey Grace."

Mrs. Coldwater shuddered. "Eamon…" she whispered, "is this true?"

"No, my dear," said Mr. Coldwater. "This child is clearly a liar."

"I ain't no liar," said Briar, her voice catching in her throat. "And they'll get in this year too. It don't matter who you put in charge—"

"Enough," said Mr. Coldwater.

"Why'd you fire my grandpa?" Briar heard her voice crack. "Grandpa Bob loves that cemetery more than anything. He took care of it all these years for you and you just let him go like he weren't nothing to you but a speck of dirt." Briar wiped her nose with the back of her sleeve. "And now he's in the hospital dying 'cause he ain't got nothing to keep him busy."

Mrs. Coldwater shot her husband a look. "Eamon, is this true?" she asked. "Did you release that good man from your service?"

Mr. Coldwater fidgeted. "Perhaps if he had accomplished the tasks he promised me—"

"Eamon Lee Coldwater," said Mrs. Coldwater, her voice rising.

"You ought to be ashamed of yourself, miserable old man. I'm certainly ashamed for you."

Mr. Coldwater's fingers danced on the head of his cane. "He promised me that he would stop the roses from coming."

"Honestly, Eamon," she said. "After all his years of service?"

"It ain't just one...*person*," said Briar. "There's loads of them sneaking in and more roses than you'll ever see in your life laid on that grave every fall."

Mrs. Coldwater gasped and covered it just as quick, her eyes welling. "Do you know why, dear? Did this, er, *friend* of yours tell you why they bring the roses?"

Briar shook her head. "He said he wouldn't never tell me. Weren't his place to speak on it." She sniffed. "But they'll come again this year. Bet your life on it."

"I hardly think so," said Mr. Coldwater. "I've been informed our new head groundskeeper seems quite keen on keeping them out."

"Nobody can stop them from getting in," said Briar. "Not Grandpa, not Jesse, not nobody. Them roses'll keep coming every year; I know it."

"How?" Mrs. Coldwater leaned forward, clasping her hands in her lap. "How do you know, dear?"

"'Cause Grandpa Bob says people mourn in all sorts of different ways," said Briar. "And it ain't right to lock folks out who need to grieve." She glared at Mr. Coldwater. "You can keep them gates locked all year round if you want, mister. It won't make a lick of difference."

"Enough of this," said Mr. Coldwater.

Briar straightened. "Most of them graves don't have nobody

come to visit them after a year or two, but them rose-givers sneak in every year because Grandpa Bob said Lainey Grace was special—"

"I said *enough*." Mr. Coldwater's hands shook as he rose from the chair.

Briar glanced at Mrs. Coldwater and saw tears in her eyes. "Wh-what's wrong?"

But Mrs. Coldwater only dabbed at her eyes with a napkin.

"Dmitri," Mr. Coldwater called.

The door swung open. "Sir?"

Mr. Coldwater pointed his silver cane at Briar without looking on her. "See this young lady to her home." He staggered back to his desk. "And warn her parents she is not allowed back or else I shall be forced to ring the police."

Briar stood before Dmitri reached her. "You ain't got to worry about me, mister. I don't plan on coming back here ever again. Just needed you to know you hurt my grandpa."

Briar walked toward the door with Dmitri falling in beside her.

"Eamon..." said Mrs. Coldwater, soft and quiet. "Eamon, you will make this right on all accounts."

Briar turned back and found Mrs. Coldwater standing.

Her husband faced her. "What did you say?"

"Don't play coy with me," she said. "You will ring that good man this very hour and offer him his job back."

"I certainly will not." Mr. Coldwater stiffened. "The others should think me weak."

"The wise among them think that already, no doubt," she said. "Honestly, what sort of person fires an old man after decades of service? Your mother would have you by the ear, if she were here, Eamon Coldwater. Aye, and drag you down to that hospital to apologize."

"Dear," said Mr. Coldwater. "Please, listen to reason—"

Mrs. Coldwater shook her head. "I don't care if all he wants is to sit behind a desk and order lunch. That man was loyal to you and, from now on, you'll be loyal to him. Do you understand me?"

Briar grinned at seeing Mr. Coldwater's chin dip like a little boy sent to the corner.

"Yes, dear," he said quietly.

"Good. Now—"

"But the gates stay locked." Mr. Coldwater's cold eyes found Briar before he turned to face the fire.

Briar smirked. *It won't matter.*

CHAPTER THIRTEEN

Flight

Briar rode her bicycle down the leafy private drive, bound for the cemetery. She glanced back and dared releasing her hold on the handlebars.

She closed her eyes and fist-pumped the air, cheering as the wind brushed against her face.

The wheel wobbled and Briar quickly took hold of its steering again.

She flew beneath the gargoyle gate and stuck her tongue out at them. Then she stood up on her pedals and coaxed more speed from the bicycle to reach the main gateway.

The oranges and reds of the horizon warned dusk approached.

Briar rode for home, thinking to stop by and tell Momma to head for the hospital. She stopped pedaling, allowing the already gathered speed to carry her, when seeing a row of cars and trucks crammed into her drive.

A pit rose in her gut as she wheeled into the drive and then the lawn to not ding up the cars. Briar dragged her feet to slow, seeing her family through the kitchen window.

Momma was wiping her eyes with tissues.

Briar dug her toes in hard, stopping the bicycle. *No.*

Daddy opened the screen door, his eyes red-stained. "Briar..."

"What's wrong?" she asked, a little voice inside her head saying she already knew. "Wh-why's everyone here, Daddy? Where's Grandpa?"

"Briar—"

"Where's Grandpa?"

Daddy glanced to the ground and his shoulders heaved before he looked up again. "He...He's gone, baby."

"No," she said, seeing Momma step outside too.

Daddy waved to her. "Come on in the house now."

"No," Briar said, wheeling the bicycle further into the lawn, tears welling in her eyes.

"Briar Ann," said Daddy as he stepped off the porch, his voice breaking. "Stop, baby."

Briar didn't. She pedaled hard to fight the grass and harder still when hearing Daddy approach. Her back tire spun when it hit the loose gravel and the handlebars wobbled in her grip, threatening to dump her.

"Russ," said Momma. "Let her go, Russ. She just needs time."

"Briar," Daddy called.

"No!" She yelled, reaching the pavement and continuing on. Anger sustained her as her legs pumped it out, driving her out of town. She closed her eyes when passing the Coldwater Cemetery, praying the bicycle would keep its straight course without veering off the side.

She didn't open her eyes again until the wheels thudded off the pavement and onto the dirt road. On and on she went, never stopping until she reached her secret spot.

The bicycle seemed to know the way, guiding itself into the ditch line.

"Trixie," Briar shouted, swinging her leg off the bicycle side and running for the culvert. "Trixie, where are you? I need my second wish!"

The leprechaun perked atop the culvert.

"*Trixie!*" Briar shouted, springing onto the culvert next to him. "I wish for you to save Grandpa Bob today...*now*."

The leprechaun's face pinched. "Lass—"

"Please, Trixie," said Briar, falling on her knees in front of him. "Please, grant my wish. I wish for Grandpa Bob to be alive and well again *today*."

Trixie's shoulders slouched. "Wish that I could, lass, but it's far too big. 'Specially for a wee leper, small as a fig."

"But you promised," she said. "You promised me a second wish this year."

"Briar—"

"*Please*," she begged through her tears. "Please, Trixie. You can have my next year's wish too. And last year's. I promise you can have them all and I won't be mad. Just bring him back. Say *granted*, Trixie. Say you'll bring him back now."

The leprechaun bowed his head. "Trixie's sorry, lass, but when someone's to be dead, not even wishes can save them from an earthly bed."

"But you have to," she said. "You just have to."

Trixie wiped tears from his eyes. "I can't—"

"Then go!" Briar snarled. "Just go! I don't need you anymore or your stupid wishes and magic! What good are they if they can't save my grandpa?"

Briar collapsed onto the culvert, sobbing. When she looked up again, Trixie was nowhere to be found.

"*Trixie*," Briar screamed. "Come back. Please, I didn't mean it. I need my second wish, Trixie. I need my—"

Her head pounded and her throat ran dry as she heaved, the pain in her soul wracking every muscle in her body.

"Grandpa," she said. "I need…I need my grandpa."

Something buzzed near her ear.

Briar swatted at the insect, missing. Then she curled up into a ball on the culvert, shaking.

"Grandpa…" she said. "Why did you have to go?"

The insect buzzed near her ear.

Briar sat up and swiped at it again. "Leave me alone!"

Though she missed, Briar glimpsed the blue-tinted wings and the long, spindly black body as it perched on the culvert's end.

The dragonfly fluttered its wings.

"Oh," said Briar. She wiped her cheeks and then reached out to touch it.

The dragonfly buzzed off the culvert, flew a circle around her, then away, the tint of its wings shimmering against the setting sun.

CHAPTER FOURTEEN

Roses

Briar squirmed outside on the cement ledge of the Wilson & Harper Funeral Home, tearing at the stiff sleeves of the dress Momma forced her to wear.

Grandpa Bob's viewing had been the night before. One of the parlor owners, Mr. Wilson himself, said he had never seen a longer line out the door of people come to pay their respects.

This morning, Briar sat alone, staring at the courthouse and the town square. She figured the tops of all the cars in the parking lot and those across the street would sparkle if only the sun would peek out. But then she guessed even the weather wanted to show it, too, mourned for Grandpa Bob.

The grey clouds had yet to break all morning and Briar swore she wouldn't be surprised if they started spitting snow soon. She shivered and blew a long breath, watching its vapor vanish.

The parlor door hinges squeaked behind her.

Briar glanced back.

Doyle stepped out into the cold, dressed in the same grey suit and off-white shirt he'd worn when inviting them to dinner. His face blustery, he took a hankie out of his pocket and honked into it, dabbing at his nostrils directly after.

"Hey, Doyle," said Briar.

The old groundskeeper's eyes widened at seeing her, though Briar thought he did his best to cover his shock. "Well, hey there, Little Miss," said Doyle. "What you doing out here? You should be inside where it's warm."

"Ain't going in 'til they close the casket," she said.

Doyle wiped his nose again. "Don't wanna see him like that, huh?"

Briar shook her head. "No, sir."

"Can't say as I blame you." Doyle approached her. He stopped just shy of the ledge and slipped off his jacket then put it around her shoulders.

"Thanks."

Doyle winked and sat down beside her, groaning as he swung his legs over the ledge. "That's why I'm out here too."

"No, it ain't," she said. "You're out here 'cause you don't want any of them in there to see you cry."

"*Huh*," he scoffed. "If Bob thinks I'm gonna shed a tear for him, he's got another thing coming. Old fart. I know he went off and died on purpose, just to spite me."

Briar gave Doyle a queer look. "Why would he do that?"

"You know how he was," said Doyle. "Always finding ways to pull aces out his sleeves. 'Classic Wade Moves,' I called them. Me and Bob been waging war all these years of card playing. Kept track of our wins on a barn wall too. 'Course he would have to go off and die when he was ahead, competitive son of a gun."

Doyle glanced skyward.

"He's up there laughing at me right now, Little Miss, I guarantee you." Doyle jerked his head toward the parlor. "Heard most people around town thought of him as the strong, silent type." Doyle crossed his arms. "Well, they ain't never played cards with him, I'll tell you that. Mild mannered, my ass."

Briar giggled.

"'Scuse my French." Doyle grinned.

"You're excused," said Briar, scooting closer to him, leaning her head on his shoulder. Her nose wrinkled at the scent of mothballs.

Doyle patted her on the back. "God, but he was a good one, wadn't he?"

Briar fought back tears at hearing the struggle in Doyle's voice. "Yessir," she said.

They embraced the quiet, just as they had many a lunch break on the tailgate of Grandpa Bob's truck when the weather felt cool enough.

Briar didn't break from Doyle until the parlor doors opened and people filed out in twos and threes—women dabbing at their eyes, men putting on a good show as they tried to keep from crying. Briar thought her heart might break when seeing the red-faced collection of aged farmers from the coffee shop.

A few patted her on the head and offered condolences. Most just walked on by.

Briar waited at Doyle's side, his jacket still wrapped around her shoulders, until she saw Daddy step out. She waved at him then wove through the crowd to reach him, hugging on his waistline.

"You ready to go in?" he asked.

Briar glanced up. "Is the casket closed?"

Daddy nodded and then ushered her inside.

Briar stepped through the doors, onto the red carpet and squeaky boards of the funeral home. Daddy led her past a wooden pulpit with a desk light and a signing book on it. Briar glanced at the yellowed pages and all the names scrawled on it when she passed by.

She swallowed hard as they zigzagged around the hall, finally reaching its end and turning the corner into the main parlor.

Rows of empty foldout chairs filled the room, spaced with only a small walkway gap down the middle of them.

Briar put her head down, not wanting to see what lay at the end, knowing she needed to. She glanced up to see metal shelves holding flower vases with little white stickers bearing the names of those who sent them. Flowered wreathes with red ribbons, small watering cans with daisies, vases with roses—Briar thought it looked like a floral shop.

But nowhere did she see any dinner-plate dahlias.

Her heart thudded when the lines of flowers tapered in toward the room's focal point and she gasped at the American flag draped over a silvery blue metal casket.

And beside the casket, propped on an easel, a framed picture of a younger Grandpa Bob. He was leaning against his work truck, arms folded across his chest, and he had a slight grin revealing the Wade dimples he'd gifted all four of his sons and their kids too.

Briar chuckled.

"Honey?" Daddy asked. "You okay?"

"Mmm-hmm. Doyle was right." Briar pointed to the picture. "Look at his grin."

"What about it?" Daddy asked.

"Classic Wade move," she said.

"Yeah," said Daddy, hugging her close.

Briar bathed in the scent of Daddy's suit that smelled like home and the minty deodorant Grandpa Bob had worn. She sighed and pulled away at the sound of squeaking boards.

Her uncles walked up the row with the funeral director, Mr. Wilson.

"Russ," said Mr. Wilson. "It's time."

Daddy nodded, then looked on Briar. "We got to take him now, baby."

She glanced at the casket. "Can I help?"

"Yeah," he said. "Not 'til we get outside though, okay?"

Briar stepped toward a wreath teeming with roses and a black ribbon down the side as Mr. Wilson and Daddy's oldest brother, Eugene, walked toward the casket.

Both men knelt and clicked the resting table's wheels unlocked while Daddy kept a hand on Grandpa Bob's casket. Then Briar's uncles lined up on either side and each placed a hand on the metal bars to either side of the casket.

Slowly, they moved forward, walking the casket and dolly it rested on.

Mr. Wilson paced over to unlock and swing open the doublewide exit doors.

Briar followed them outside as the Wade men tread carefully

down the ramp and turned the corner toward the waiting black hearse. Briar ran down the ramp as Mr. Wilson opened the hearse's back door to accept the casket.

She joined Daddy near the back end and clasped her hand on a casket rail then winced under the shared weight of it.

Her oldest uncles guided the front of the casket onto the hearse rails. Then, one by one, each Wade pallbearer stepped away.

Daddy pushed the back end until it lay fully inside the hearse, then Mr. Wilson gently closed the door and pushed on the door until it clicked.

That's that. Briar thought it was something Grandpa Bob would say of such things.

She turned to follow Daddy back to his truck, already parked in the funeral lineup. Briar expected them to be fourth in line, being that he was the youngest of the four Wade brothers, but Daddy's truck was fifth, behind some stranger's car.

Briar stopped. "Daddy," she pointed. "That's not their place in line. That's yours."

"It's all right, Briar," he said, taking her by the arm. "It's just a spot in line is all. Dad didn't know any strangers."

Briar hesitated. "But it ain't right."

Daddy sighed. "Come get in the truck, baby."

"But, Daddy—"

"I said get in the truck." Daddy's face flushed. *"Now."*

Her nostrils flared as she marched toward their place in line, making sure to sneer at the stranger.

Momma had the heat already running as both Briar and Daddy climbed inside the truck.

Briar buckled her seat belt and then stared out the windshield at the red Chrysler parked in front of them.

"It ain't right, Daddy," she said. "Grandpa would say—"

"Briar Ann," Daddy snapped, his stern gaze finding hers in the rearview mirror. "I done told you to knock it off already. We ain't got time for this today. Now you hush up about it. Just a place in line is all. It don't mean nothing."

"But—"

"*Hey!*" Daddy wheeled around and slapped the seat, his face twisted in anger. "I said knock it off."

Briar shrank, looking to Momma for rescue, finding none. She felt her lip quiver, but nodded to Daddy. Then she looked out the window to keep from crying and didn't tear her gaze away until they reached the cemetery.

Daddy put the truck in park and turned off the key. He climbed outside and slammed the door without waiting on either Briar or Momma.

Briar watched him through the windshield, striding on toward the hearse.

"Ain't you gonna help them?" Momma asked.

"He don't want my help," she said.

"That's not true," said Momma, gathering Kleenexes inside her purse. "Your daddy loves you, darlin'. More than anything in this whole wide world."

"Then why'd he yell at me?" she asked. "I was trying to stick up for him. Everyone knows it's supposed to be family first. Grandpa would say—"

"Briar Ann," said Momma. "It's over."

Not to me, Briar thought, glancing out the window.

Mr. Wilson and Doyle hustled to unload all the flowers and wreaths from the funeral parlor and carry them to the graveside. Then Daddy and the others unloaded Grandpa Bob's casket and bore it toward the large wintergreen, tented canopy.

See. Briar thought. *Didn't wanna wait on me to help.*

"Come on now," said Momma, opening her door. "It's time."

Briar crawled outside. She didn't miss the scathing look Momma gave her either when forgetting to exit like a lady. Briar fumed all the way up the grass pathway to burial space thirty-three.

She followed Momma into the tent and sat in one of the newer, (and cheaper, Grandpa Bob had called them) white-washed plastic chairs that sunk under her.

Briar stared on the American flag and the casket while the preacher droned on and on with the same passage she had heard him use at countless other burials. To keep from falling asleep, she looked through the back tent opening and scouted all the trees in sight, not seeing a single leaf on any of them.

They'll be coming soon, Grandpa, she thought, turning her attention back to the casket. *You might have just missed them.*

Briar wondered where Trixie had got off to and when he might return to grant her second wish. Not that she knew what to wish for, now that Grandpa Bob was gone.

She leaned forward in her chair when the honor guard raised their rifles and trained their aim skyward, firing off the first of three volleys. Briar covered her ears when the bugler put his instrument to his lips and performed "Taps."

After the preacher gave the final prayer, Briar sat up to watch the familiar VFW honor guard remove the American flag from

Grandpa Bob's casket, their movements careful not to let any part of it touch the ground. Then they folded it over and again, until it formed a triangle with the stars showing.

Almost looks like a paper football, Briar thought when they handed over the flag to her oldest uncle, Eugene.

The crowd retreated to their cars, off to the Methodist church where the ladies had undoubtedly worked all morning preparing a meal. Then everyone would tell stories and catch up with one another.

Briar stayed behind with Daddy and her uncles.

Each of the four Wade brothers had worked in the cemetery at one point or another, and, since one of them owned the vault company, they each took a hand in helping prepare Grandpa Bob's casket for his final resting place.

The concrete vault—a hollowed and hulking bronze cover likened to a sarcophagus in the mummy stories Briar read about—hung poised over the casket by a pair of cables at either end attached to aluminum rigging.

Briar saw the name Robert Wade etched on a nameplate outside the vault's casing. *But his name was Bob,* she thought. *Why don't it say Bob?*

Uncle Dusty turned the hand crank to lower the vault lid over the casket, while the other brothers guided it down to ensure the vault sealed.

Uncle Alan folded back the green blanket cover, revealing the fat belts the crew had laid before the vault base was set down on it. Each son took hold of a belt end and clipped it to the winch rigging above. The hand crank turned again, raising the vault off the pedestal, suspending it to allow Briar's uncles and Daddy to remove a row of boards—all that stood between Grandpa Bob and the grave.

Get in there and help. Briar stepped in and took one of the boards away, each one removed revealing more of the darkened burial hole.

Daddy looked up at her. "You wanna see something?"

Briar nodded.

"Look right there," he pointed to a bit of the earthen wall, lighter in tone than the rest. "Know what that is?"

"Grandma's vault," said Briar, recalling the first time Grandpa Bob had called her over to show her just such a thing. "We gonna lay his down in beside hers, right?"

"Yep." Daddy glanced at his brothers. "Ready?"

Briar backed away at their nod.

The crank turned slowly, easing the head groundskeeper's vault into its final resting place.

Briar leaned against Daddy, forgetting her anger with him when he kissed the top of her head.

"Whoa, Dusty," said Uncle Eugene. "It's there."

The vault crew guided the belts back out, then rolled them back onto the pole like thread on a spool.

Briar glanced to the blue tarp covering the mound of dirt dug up to make the burial hole. Then she knelt and picked up a handful of dirt, sprinkling it atop Grandpa Bob's vault.

"Come on, Briar Ann," said Daddy. "It's time to go."

Briar's gaze fell on the rows of flowers and wreaths, her eyes drawn to the largest of them all—a silver vase teeming with deep, crimson roses.

"Daddy," she tugged on his sleeve. "Who brought those?"

"I dunno."

Doyle ambled over and poked his hand around, moving the roses in search of a nametag or sticker. He shrugged. "Guess someone didn't want us to know."

Briar sighed and walked to the vase, feeling the petals between her fingers. "Can we take them, Daddy?"

"No, baby. Someone else will load all these up. We need to get to the church for the meal."

"I'll load them—"

Briar's lip curled at the voice behind her.

"Ain't got nowhere else to be."

Paycheck worker, she thought, glaring at Jesse Thomason.

She hadn't noticed him among the crowd before because he looked a whole new man to her: clean-shaven, his hair washed and combed over, and wearing a brown suit that Briar thought looked like something out of a 70's disco movie.

Jesse moved to pick up the first vase.

"No," said Briar, moving to stop him.

"What?" Jesse asked. "What's wrong?"

"I said no."

Daddy came to her side. "What's a matter?"

"Don't let him take these, Daddy," she said. "He'll burn them." Jesse's face paled.

"He burned Lainey Grace's roses!" she shouted, backing away. "That's what he does—"

Jesse shook his head. "I—"

"You're a paycheck worker, Jesse Thomason." Briar spit. "He don't got no respect for nothing! He burns roses on account of he ain't got no one and he's—"

"That's enough!" Daddy thundered, grabbing hold of Briar's arm.

She spun free of his grip, dropping the vase to clatter on the ground, then sprinted across the cemetery.

CHAPTER FIFTEEN

Second Wish

Briar ran at the tree near the grave of Lainey Grace.

"Why?" she screamed, punching the tree. "Why don't he take my side?" She hit it again, bleeding her knuckles. "Why don't he ever believe me?"

Briar collapsed, sobbing. She brushed back her hair with both hands, scratching her scalp, hoping to stop the pounding in her head.

A falling leaf tickled her neck.

Briar slapped at it, but she caught only air.

The leaf tickled her again.

Briar spun around.

Trixie dropped the dangled leaf he held and climbed up the tree, laughing.

"What are you doing?" Briar asked.

"Me? What about ye, lass? Why ye down in the dumps? Keep this up longer, and I'll start calling ye Grumps."

"Stop it," she said, standing up and walking away. "I'm not in the mood."

"That's no fun. I don't like down and dreary. What can Trixie do, to make ye more cheery?"

"I just want him to be...ugh." Briar paced the cemetery lawn. "I just wish he would be nicer."

"Who?" asked Trixie.

Someone cleared their throat behind her. "Beg your pardon."

Briar turned. "Jesse?"

His face pinched, Jesse held one of the crimson roses in his hand, the stem broken.

Briar thought he looked about to speak. Then she heard another voice whisper.

"*Granted.*"

Briar's eyes widened. "No!" She spun to look around the mound and glanced up the tree.

The leprechaun stood in the crook of a branch, near a squirrel hole.

"Trixie!" Briar called. "Wait. That wasn't my wish. Please!"

But the leprechaun only winked and thumbed his nose at her. Then he donned his hood and dashed into the hole, laughing.

Briar ran at the tree, striking the bark. "Trixie! Come back."

"Who you yelling at?" Jesse asked.

"Ugh." Briar kicked the tree trunk. "I *hate* leprechauns and their stupid games!"

"Leprechauns," said Jesse. "Right..."

"What are you doing here?" She slumped against the tree.

Jesse shrugged. "Don't rightly know, I guess. Asked your daddy and them if it'd be all right if I came to talk with you."

"So why are you looking for me?" Briar asked. "Come to tell me off on the day I bury my grandpa?"

Jesse knelt and picked up a bit of clover, twirling it between his fingertips. "No. Came to tell you that you's wrong about me." He allowed the wind blow the clover away. "Well, little bit of both I reckon. I ain't been the gentlest dog in the yard. But I...I'm changing."

"You can't," she said. "Grandpa Bob told me you was a pay-check worker. Can't nobody teach that out of you."

"He taught it out of me," said Jesse. "Er, tried to anyway."

"What do you mean?"

"Look," said Jesse. "I know you ain't got no reason to trust me."

"And I don't," she said.

Jesse nodded. "Might be I could show you something that would change that." He offered her the rose. "If you wanna see, that is."

Briar squinted. "Tell me."

Jesse shook his head. "You wouldn't believe me. Got to show you. It's the only way you'll know for certain."

Briar looked across the yard, wondering where Daddy and her uncles might be.

Something small struck her in the head.

"Ow!" said Briar, seeing an acorn near her foot. She glanced up to the tree.

Trixie had poked his head out, his mischievous grin broadening. He pointed to the equipment barn then tucked back into the squirrel hole.

"What you looking at?" Jesse asked, turning.

Not everything is as it seems, Briar thought. She swallowed her pride and fears. "Show me."

"It's in the equipment barn," he said. "Up in the hayloft."

Briar scratched her neck. "Grandpa Bob said I ain't supposed to go up there."

"You ever wonder why?" Jesse stepped to the grave of Lainey Grace and laid his rose atop it. "Now's your chance to find out."

Briar felt a lump in her stomach. She nodded anyway. "Okay... I'll go with you."

"All right then," said Jesse, waving. "Come on."

Briar followed him, noticing he didn't attempt to outpace her like he had in summers past. Jesse even caught her when she tripped in the stupid dress heels Momma had forced her wear.

Trixie. Briar grimaced. *It's gotta be the wish. Jesse's never been this nice to me.*

Briar focused on the white equipment barn as they walked out the main gateway and Jesse turned right to cut across the backyard. She never once glanced at Grandpa Bob's former house.

Jesse bent low as they walked past the house and scooped up a dandelion, ripping it out and tossing it. "I try to keep the yard and the house nice, like he did. You can go in and see if you—"

"No," said Briar. "I don't ever need to go in there again. I wanna remember it like it was."

"Ain't changed much," said Jesse. "He didn't have a lot, and I don't neither."

Briar pointed to the sliding barn door. "You left it open."

"Yeah, I forget sometimes," he said. "*Most* times, to hear Doyle tell it. I'm getting better though."

Jesse walked inside the barn and headed for the creaky, wooden stairwell.

Briar followed him up, hesitating when one of the boards squealed louder than the others.

"Watch out for this next one," said Jesse, pointing. "I still need to put another nail in, else it's liable to fall through."

He offered her his hand.

Briar looked at the loose step and the distance to the next one higher up. Frowning, she took hold of Jesse's hand.

He yanked her up to the next step then climbed the last of them with Briar behind him.

The barn's second floor held an assortment of equipment— various sized forming boards to help set a headstone, wooden paddles for tamping earth to pack loose dirt in, empty grass seed sacks.

Jesse tread across the wood plank floor, onto the built-in ladder that led to the hayloft. "I'll climb up first, if you wanna wait here," he said.

"Ain't you gonna flick that light on?"

"Not 'til you get up there."

"How come?" Briar asked.

"You'll see."

Briar stood back, watching the dust fall from the soles of his shoes as he ascended. More filtered through the cracks in the wood planks once he reached the loft and walked around.

"Come on up," said Jesse.

Briar reached for the ladder. *Well, Grandpa did say never to go up alone,* she reasoned.

She took the first rung then hurried to take another. Up the ladder she went, dizzied by the height, fueled with a need to know what lay in the loft.

Briar peeked her head over the floorboards. Finishing her climb, she stood on the landing and wiped her dirty hands on her dress.

"You ready to see?" he asked.

"I'm ready."

The lights flicked on.

Briar gasped.

Row after row of bundled roses dangled from the rafters. Thousands of roses, their petals dried and crisped, their hues darkened from their original shades.

"Grandpa..." said Briar, her gaze wandering from each rafter to the next, the scent clotting up her nose. "He saved them."

"All but them right there," Jesse pointed to the fourth rafter. "Them's the ones I hung last year."

Briar's gaze dropped to Jesse. "You saved them?"

Jesse nodded. "Didn't seem right to burn them like Uncle Ted wanted me to, not after how tore up I saw you were last year 'fore you lit out." Jesse hopped from beam to beam and stood under the fourth row of roses, looking up at them. "Asked your grandpa and Doyle what I should do with them. Since he was already fired and Uncle Ted couldn't hurt him no more, Bob brought me up here and showed me."

Jesse chuckled.

"Guess whenever my uncle Ted came round and ordered him bag up those new roses from the grave of Lainey Grace, why, Bob and Doyle would bring them bags up here, bundle the roses up, and string them upside down to keep the petals on."

Jesse pointed to an empty rafter.

"Said every year in the winter, just before a good snow was coming in, why, he'd come up here and grab him all them bundles from a few years back and take them out to spread the dried rose petals over Lainey's grave, just to make sure she still had what belonged to her. You believe that?"

Briar nodded. "I do."

"Yeah, I reckon you do." Jesse sighed. "Bob was good to me. I ain't gonna deny we had our share a disagreements. But—"

Briar turned toward him, hearing his voice crack.

Jesse glanced away. "Your grandpa taught me a lot, is what I'm trying to say."

Briar's shoulders heaved when Jesse dared look at her, unable to hide the glistening in his eyes.

"Ain't, uh…" Jesse sniffed. "Ain't never had no one try to teach me like he did. Even that day he turned the key to his house over to me, Bob said he weren't mad. Just asked me to take care of it and these grounds for him. Do what he taught me to do."

Briar nodded, wiping her cheeks. "That sounds like Grandpa."

"What you said out by his grave, 'bout me burning Lainey Grace's roses, well…" Jesse looked at his feet. "Guess I just needed you to know that I'm trying, is all."

Briar glanced on the roses.

"Maybe then you, at least…" Jesse hesitated. "Well, maybe you could see what little good he saw in me. I know I ain't never gonna be as good a man or groundskeeper as Bob, but—"

Briar threw her arms around Jesse, staining his suit with her tears. "I'm sorry, Jesse," she said.

"Me too," he choked, hugging her back. "Wish it hadn't ended up like this. Wished I hadn't a stormed out that night being all mad at him. It's just this temper, I got. Thought maybe him and Doyle was playing another prank on me, trying to get me not to wait inside by the grave of Lainey Grace and catch them. But now that he's gone, I…"

Jesse looked up at the rafters.

"I'm scared there ain't gonna be no more roses to bundle up." His chin quivered. "Y'all ain't the only ones look forward to seeing them round her grave every fall."

"They'll be there again," said Briar. "Just you wait."

"Wish I could believe that," said Jesse.

"They will be," she said. "You'll see."

"I hope you're right."

Briar nodded. "That mean you're not gonna wait inside the cemetery?"

Jesse shook his head. "Don't seem right to. Whoever it is, I don't mean to scare them off this year." He stepped away from her. "You think, uh, you think Lainey Grace'd mind if we took one of these bundles and mixed them petals up with the dirt for Bob's grave?"

"No," said Briar. "I think she'd feel that was just right."

Jesse smiled. "Me too."

He fetched a ladder leaning against the barn side then climbed up to take down a bundle.

Briar descended the ladder from the loft and then looked up to receive the bundle Jesse handed her.

"Careful," he said. "They still got thorns on them."

Briar stepped back up on the ladder for a better handoff. Then she waited for Jesse to come down.

They walked out of the barn together, Briar carrying the roses back to the cemetery, and then on toward Grandpa Bob's open grave.

Daddy and his brothers stood around it with Doyle, the lot of them filling the dirt in together. None of them said a word about the bundle of roses or asked where she got it.

Briar guessed each of them knew.

She tore off a couple petals, listening to their crunch, and tossed them onto the vault. Then she handed the bundle down the line, allowing Doyle, Jesse, and all Grandpa Bob's sons to do the same.

"All right then, boys," said Doyle, leaning on his shovel as his tears flowed without care or concern for who saw. "Let's get to."

Briar took up her own shovel, helping Daddy and her uncles and the two cemetery groundskeepers honor Grandpa Bob. They only halted long enough to allow Daddy to hop down and tamp the dirt with what looked a boat oar, ensuring there weren't any air pockets to settle the vault askew. Then they took up their shovels again, repeating the laborious process until finishing the work.

Briar held onto her shovel even after the last bit of dirt was spread, the ache in her arms nothing compared to that in her soul.

Something chirped in a nearby row—a ground squirrel, or so it looked, peeking around one of the headstones.

"Trixie..." Briar said quietly. She gave her shovel to Doyle and walked toward the headstone Trixie hid behind.

The leprechaun grinned and ducked away at her approach.

Briar stepped around the headstone and found him gone,

but he had left a gift behind: a single rose, its petals glittering green and tipped with gold.

Briar picked up the rose.

She glanced around the cemetery, scouting every naked tree.

Briar twirled the rose stem between her fingers. Her grin dawned as the petals fluttered, and a single thought danced in her mind.

Tonight.

CHAPTER SIXTEEN

The *Other* Groundskeeper

Briar looked up at the pair of dangling roses she'd hung over her bed. *I know what's real,* she thought, staring at the newest rose Trixie had left her.

She turned and glanced at the bedside clock—*10 p.m.*

The house had been quiet for a couple hours now, Daddy having gone to bed as soon as they got home. But Briar knew Momma had only been in bed about an hour and she never slept all night long.

Not like Daddy. Once he was out, he was dead to the world.

Briar slipped out of bed and put on her cemetery workpants. They fit a little snugger than she remembered, but she bore the extra tightness all the same. Then she rolled up a second pair of socks and laced up her heavy boots before donning a hoodie and layering her Carhartt jacket over it.

She eased open the window and slipped outside into the cool air and full moonlight.

Briar tumbled into the lawn, rolling to her feet, and fetching her bicycle out from behind the bushes. She swung astride it and pushed off. Rather than risk being seen by any police that might be out patrolling, Briar rode straight for the town culvert.

The creek was low after an uncommonly arid summer and she wheeled her bicycle down the hill onto the nearly dry embankment. She plucked her front wheel out of the muck, then slowly found firmer ground and rode onward until no security lights glowed near the roadside.

Briar swung off the bicycle and walked it up out of the creek. She grimaced when finding her surroundings near the old railroad tracks that once ran through the cemetery.

Too far east.

She followed the track lines up a short distance until they ended, squished, it seemed, by the looming cemetery wall.

"Dang it," said Briar, looking around the surrounding woods and fields. *Have to go around.*

An owl hooted in the woods.

Briar ignored its warning and continued on anyway.

"Trixie," she called out, loud as she dared. "Trixie, where are you?"

She cursed when he didn't appear.

Probably already inside with his friends, she thought. *Or else he knows I'm mad at him for tricking me with that second wish.*

Briar continued on, wheeling her bicycle along the ivy wall, staring up at the night sky. "Grandpa," she said. "If you're up there, I could sure use some help right now."

She thought one of the stars twinkled.

The wind picked up, shrieking through the trees.

Briar winced and steered toward the weeds. She jumped off, leaving her bicycle, and cowered next to a knotted tree trunk.

"Please, stop," she begged.

The wind quieted, replaced by something different.

Briar uncovered her ears, sitting up. *What was that?*

A low rumble wandered over the horizon.

"Dang..."

Briar glanced at the cloudless sky. *But it can't be thunder then.*

The rumble occurred again. *"Dang..."*

Briar grabbed up her bicycle from the weeds.

That's not thunder! She pushed the bicycle toward the voice.

"Oh, shoot," the deep voice drawled louder.

Briar saw a snaky shadow fly into the air, landing atop the ivy wall, then fall away without catching hold.

"Dang..." A bulky shadow moved between the cemetery's ivy wall and the forest tree line. One of its limbs seemed to swing upward and let fly a rope with a hook on its end.

Briar crouched near the tree line and saw the roped hook again catch some ivy on the cemetery wall then fall away.

"Forget it." The lumpy shadow gave up its attempts and turned to the forest. "The fairies can fly it over."

Fairies? Briar started forward, concern drawing over her face that she might lose sight of the shadow.

"Stupid wall." The shadow sighed and sat down. "Stupid gates."

Briar felt a small quake in her feet. She crept steadily forward until she saw not a shadow, but a creature. Seated, she guessed him at around eight feet tall with thick, muscular limbs and bluish-green skin.

Whoa. Briar thought. *How tall would he be if he was standing up?*

His pants looked hand stitched from fifty burlap sacks, with holes in the knees, and he wore a belt of tattered rope ends knotted together. His sleeveless shirt was a patchwork mess of threadbare horse blankets and red, Farmall tractor covers.

Coarse, black hair covered his arms and cheeks, though it was cropped low atop his head. His nose looked like a bulbous mushroom attached to a boulder. His big doe eyes dominated his face, brown and deep-set.

He's a troll! Briar beamed.

The owl hooted again from somewhere in the forest.

The troll's eyes went wide in search. "Wh-who's there?" he asked.

A tawny owl swooped low out of the trees with Trixie on its back.

The leprechaun guided the owl to earth then jumped off, rolling as he hit the ground, then hopping up. Trixie spun and made a bow, swooping off his hood. "Why it's just me again, ye big, scaredy lout. Did ye come all this way to help Trixie out?"

"No," said the troll. "Not ever again. You tricked me in our eating contest. The fauns told me how you beat me."

Trixie shrugged then shook his finger up at the troll. "I warned ye don't test me. Aye, ye dig your own holes. Next time you'll be sure, I don't switch out the bowls."

"Huh," said the troll. "So where's your faun friends tonight?"

"Only brought the one, she hides by that tree. One look at you, heh. I'm surprised she don't flee." Trixie turned and stared squarely at Briar. "Come out, little Briar. Aye, I know that you heard. I got you a new friend here, in this big troll, Ferd."

Briar strode out from the tree line. "*You!*" she pointed at Trixie. "You tricked me again! You made me waste my second wish."

"Wasted?" Trixie huffed. "How's that? Ye can't be that blind. Not now that Jesse's much nicer I find."

The leprechaun laughed at her pouting.

"You little schemer." Briar ran at him.

But Trixie only laughed harder and ran for the ivy, climbing faster than Briar's eyes followed.

"Trixie!" she yelled. "Come back here. I wanna unlock the gates. Grant my first wish!"

Trixie twirled his curly, crimson hair. "One day I will, lass. Aye, we'll go on a grand tour. But to do it tonight"—Trixie winked—"t'would cheapen the allure."

"Trixie!"

"So farewell for now, lass." Trixie made another sweeping bow. "Aye, farewell 'til next fall. If ye need anything now, ye give Ferd a call."

The leprechaun dashed over the ivy wall, cackling.

"Urgh!" Briar stomped her feet. "I hate leprechauns!"

"Yeeeeah," the troll drawled. "He does that to people. I never liked leprechauns much either, mostly cause I can't catch them."

Briar gulped as she stared up at the troll.

The troll's cheeks flushed bluer and he grinned a big, dopey grin, filled with crooked, stained teeth. "Hi…"

Briar chuckled. "Hi."

"Who are you?" he asked.

"I'm Briar."

The troll grinned wider still and pointed to a white seed bag that had been sewn over his left breast pocket, with a name stenciled in blue, cursive writing.

Fred, Briar read the name.

"I'm Ferd," he said.

Briar's grin faded. "But your nametag says Fred."

"It does?" The troll's forehead wrinkled, bringing the warts closer together. He tugged at the shirt, staring down on the nametag. He sighed. "Oh, shoot."

"What's wrong?" Briar asked.

The troll sniffled and raised a giant hand, wiping his eye. "I always get the letters mixed up when I try to read."

"At least you know how." Briar stepped closer. "So is it Ferd or Fred?"

"Ferd...that's what everyone calls me at least." He glanced down at the nametag. "Or maybe it's Fred...I don't know."

Briar choked back a laugh. "Did someone teach you to read then, Ferd?"

"Yeah...a long time ago," he said. "Lainey Grace taught me."

Briar's eyes widened. "You knew Lainey Grace?"

Ferd nodded. "She never poked fun at me either, like them others." He tugged on his sleeve. "And she made this shirt special for me cause don't no others fit."

"It's a nice shirt," said Briar.

"Yeah..." He blushed again. "I try to do something special for her every year, but it don't never turn out right." Ferd looked at the ivy wall. "Not that it matters, I guess. Can't get inside anyway with this wall here."

"Well, you're big and strong," said Briar. "You could probably knock it down, if you wanted to."

"Oh no," he said, looking around the forest as if someone might hear her. "I wouldn't ever try that. Lainey wouldn't want me to."

"Why not?"

Ferd clapped a hand over his mouth.

"What's wrong?" Briar asked.

Ferd shook his head.

"Come on," said Briar. "You can tell me."

His big shoulders heaved. "We're not supposed to talk about her. Not our place to speak on her story."

"But why?" Briar pouted. "Why can't you or Trixie tell me more about her? Why do you and all the others bring the roses?"

"The roses!" Ferd climbed to his feet. "Oh, shoot."

"What?" asked Briar, watching him head for the woods. "What's wrong?"

"They'll be here soon," he said. "And most can't get in without me."

Briar's spirit soared with the thought she might meet other fantastical creatures soon.

Ferd groaned near the tree line and returned a moment later with a stack of plywood on his shoulder.

How's he carrying that? Briar wondered. *He needs a crane!*

"What's with all the wood?" she asked.

"Have to wait and find out." Ferd chuckled as if he'd said the funniest thing ever heard. Then he bent at the knees, took a deep breath, and grunted as he heaved up, tossing the stack toward the ivy wall as if he launched a shotput weight.

"Wha…." Briar uttered.

The plywood stack unfolded and, like a magic trick deck of

cards glued together, snapped together as one to form a long, sheeted ramp that fell across the ground.

"I know what you're thinking," said Ferd, as he ambled toward the ivy wall and the head of the plywood ramp.

Briar shrugged.

"I got to get me one of those."

Ferd chuckled again at his own joke. He knelt by the plywood and got his fingers under it, then hoisted it up over his head, and walked under the ramp, hand over hand, his biceps trembling.

Briar stepped back as the ramp end rose higher up the ivy wall, the ropes that had tied the stack together now dangling.

"Is it...at the...top yet?" Ferd asked, struggling under the weight of the lofted end.

"You're almost there," said Briar. "Keep going!"

He grunted and heaved again, taking another step. Then another.

"You got it!" Briar shouted, as the ramp end teetered higher than the ivy. "It's above the wall."

Ferd sighed and, with a final heave of his massive shoulders, brought the ramp back to rest its top on the wall.

"You did it, Ferd."

"I had a good helper." He beamed down at her.

Briar rested her head against his leg and felt the palm of his hand on her back, nudging her forward. She glanced up into his big brown eyes. "What?"

Ferd pointed to the ramp. "What are you waiting for? It'll hold," he said. "Go ahead."

Briar giggled and ran for it, sprinting to the top, ever drawing nearer to the full moon as her feet thundered up the wooden floor and she saw the ramp also ran down the other side. She hesitated atop the wall, the Coldwater Cemetery stretching beneath her like a miniature movie model.

Briar thought of Emma then, wondering if she'd seen such a sight in California yet. "Nope," she said to the night, her gaze training on the winding path toward the one place she wanted to go. "California ain't got the grave of Lainey Grace."

Briar clapped at the gathered shadows around the grave and Trixie's cackled laugh in the vicinity. *I found them, Grandpa Bob. I found their way in.*

She peered over the wall, down the thirty feet drop.

Vertigo took hold of her, and Briar stepped back.

"Ferd," she said, turning.

The big troll looked up at her from his ground, his big eyes shining.

Briar's face pinched. "You're not coming?"

"Ramp won't hold me," said Ferd. "I'm too big."

Briar took a step down the ramp. "But..."

"It's all right," he said. "I get to help the others sneak in. Sometimes that's got to be enough, I suppose."

Briar heard him sigh from all the way up on the wall. "Ain't you ever gone inside the cemetery?" she asked.

"Nope." he said. "Sure would like too though. Maybe someday, I will. 'Til then, I just haul the ramp back and forth every fall."

"But, that's not fair."

"It is what it is." Ferd shrugged. "Hey, do you know why they lock them gates? Is it to keep the dead inside?"

"No," Briar choked. "My grandpa said it was to keep the living out."

"Yeah," said Ferd, his chin dropping to his chest as he shook his big head. "That's what I thought."

Briar glanced over the wall at the cemetery, her thoughts drifting to Daddy and the funeral lineup.

She turned and ran back down the ramp, careful not to stumble all the way down.

"Wh-what are you doing?" Ferd asked.

"I ain't going in," she said.

"Well, why not?"

"It ain't right," she said, throwing herself against him, her arms not reaching a quarter of the way around him. "It ain't right if I get to go in and you don't. Not when you been coming here all these years having to watch everyone else pass by."

Ferd sniffled. "That's mighty kind of you."

She beamed up at him. "So how do you get your rose on the grave of Lainey Grace?"

"Oh, usually I just give it to—" Ferd's jaw hung open. He slouched, blowing hot steam on her face that reeked of mushrooms. "Oh, shoot…"

"What?" she asked, waving the scent away. "What's wrong?"

"I forgot again," he said. "Forgot my rose at home."

"Well, how far away is it?" Briar asked. "Do we have time to go back?"

Ferd looked up at the moon, squinting. "Maybe…Yeah. Might be we could make it back in time. 'Specially seeing as there's no one here yet." He glanced at Briar. "You wanna come with me? I can carry you."

Ferd laid the back of his hand on the ground, opening his palm to her.

Briar grinned and stepped onto his hand, wobbling to keep her balance as he scooped her up and slid her into his left breast pocket.

Is this what it feels like being Trixie? Briar wondered. She settled in, draping her arms and chin over the pocket sleeve, then glanced up at Ferd. "Where are we going?"

"Huh," he said. "You'll see."

CHAPTER SEVENTEEN

Winter Storage

Briar swayed back and forth in Ferd's pocket, listening to his deep, rumbled breaths, as he wandered deeper into the woods.

He glanced down on her, his eyes the size of dinner plates. "Sorry for the bumpy ride," he said.

"It's all right," said Briar, wincing when he took another hard step. "Is something wrong with your legs?"

"Mmm-hmm," said Ferd. "The witch-doctor ain't never figured out whether one of my legs was too long, or the other was too short."

Briar laughed. "My grandpa would call that a hitch in your giddyup," she said. "He had one too."

Ferd stopped. "Heh," he said. "I thought I was the only one."

"Nope," she said. "He had trouble walking too sometimes. Said his feet felt like concrete blocks."

"Mine do too." Ferd started walking again. "Sometimes I'm afraid they'll never stop growing."

"I don't think I'll ever grow taller," she said.

"You will," said Ferd.

Briar leaned back against his big chest, feeling his pulse thunder under his shirt, listening to the thuds as he walked.

She never felt her eyelids droop, but found Ferd looking at the stars when she woke up. Briar was lying in his palm, as he'd plucked her out of his pocket while she was asleep.

"Ferd," she said, yawning and stretching. "Where are we?"

The big troll looked down on her. "We're here."

Briar stood up and took in her surroundings. "But this..." she trailed, as she stepped off his palm and onto a dry bank of Newman Creek. "This is my secret spot."

The culvert lay before her, its darkened maw gaped wide.

"Oh," said Ferd. "No one told me that. Guess I'll just get my stuff and move on then..."

"No." Briar reached her hand to stop him.

But Ferd lumbered under the culvert anyway.

"Wait," she said, running into the dark after him. "Ferd! Ferd, where are you?"

"In here," his voice echoed through the culvert.

"I can't see you," said Briar.

"Oh, right," said Ferd.

Briar heard a deep throaty sound, the pitch rising and falling. *He...he's humming.*

The metal culvert shimmered blue, just as Briar had seen it do when the creek waters ran under it. The metal brightened and shone all the more brilliantly when Ferd kept up his tune. Within moments, the whole culvert inside gleamed as if frost-covered in a deep freeze.

"Ferd," she said. "H-how did you do this?"

"Troll magic," he said, wandering further in toward the culvert middle.

Briar followed Ferd as he felt along, his fingers brushing between the rivets, muttering under his breath.

"Ah," he said. "Here we are."

He leaned against the metal siding and pushed.

Briar jumped back when a door swung inward against an earthen wall.

"Oops." Ferd stepped away, his hand holding open the door. "Sorry about that. Didn't mean to scare you. Wanna come inside?"

Briar peered around him, through the doorway.

She saw an earthen hall, tall and wide enough to accommodate Ferd, lined with roots that shimmered like blue-gold veins all the way down.

Briar beamed and nodded at Ferd. "Yes, please."

"Okay, then," said Ferd, straightening. "Ladies first."

Briar started forward and stepped through the open rivet door. The dirt floor was solid and packed tight and she ran her fingers along the earthen wall, tracing the roots as she descended.

The ceiling rose when the hall ended, mounding in a dome with the dirt ceiling braced back by sprawling roots. There was a stone workbench and bed and shelves carved out of the earth. Briar approached one shelf littered with dried, crunchy rose petals and a smoothed piece of driftwood that had a charcoal sketch of Ferd on it.

Briar picked up the piece, her eyes drawn to the initials L.G. scribbled in the lower right side.

"She made that for me," said Ferd.

Briar sat the driftwood piece back on the shelf. "It's beautiful," she said.

"Yeah," said Ferd. "I try to do something for her every year, only—"

"It don't turn out right?" Briar asked.

"Hey," he said. "How'd you know that?"

"You told me already," she said, grinning. "You big troll."

Ferd smiled back. "Okay, then. Guess I'll just find my rose then and we'll go back. Getting late already." He scratched his head. "Or early. I never can remember which."

He shuffled around his home.

Briar wandered around, out of his way, touching the hollow stone bowls on one shelf, then arrowheads and smooth, skipping stones he had collected on another.

"Dang." Ferd sighed. "Where'd I put it?"

Briar smirked and continued exploring. She found empty glass bottles resting on a thick tree root, leaning against the earth wall, separated by brand as if Ferd meant to keep stock of each and every one.

Then she saw a small box, crafted of twigs with mossy ends peeking out through the gaps, and a flat piece of driftwood lain atop it as a lid.

Briar glanced over her shoulder at Ferd, still rooting around in a corner of the home, muttering. She turned back to the box and slowly lifted the driftwood lid.

A black thing buzzed out quickly.

Briar fell back, yelping.

"What's wrong?" Ferd asked. "What happ—Oh."

Briar turned around. "I'm sorry, Ferd. I didn't—"

"It's okay," he said, reaching toward the ceiling and opening his palm. "Come here, little guy. That's right. Come here."

Briar stood.

"There you go," said Ferd, collecting it in his palm. "That's better, right?"

"What is it?" she asked, stepping closer.

"Oh, it's nothing really." Ferd brought his hand for her to see.

Briar covered her mouth, seeing what rested in his palm.

The dragonfly fluttered its blue-tinted wings.

"They die in the winter if they ain't got no place to go." Ferd smiled and ran his stubby finger along its back. "I catch as many as I can and keep them down here with me 'til spring."

Ferd gently nudged the dragonfly back into the box and covered it back up with the lid.

"Did you—" Briar sniffled and dabbed her eyes. "Did you find your rose?"

"Yeah," he said. "It's over there, if you wanna take a look."

Briar found the withered rose bush planted inside a black, plastic flowerpot on the stone bed. It yielded but a single, dead blossom with black thorns and molded petals.

"I killed it again," said Ferd. "Didn't I?"

"I think so." Briar touched its yellowed leaves. "Did you put Epsom salt on it?"

"Huh?"

Briar shrugged. "That's what Grandpa Bob would ask people who wanted to know about roses. He'd always tell them to put Epsom salt on it."

"Where do you get that?"

"I could probably find some," she said. "Well, not tonight. But maybe you can use them in the spring."

"Okay," he said, reaching for the flowerpot. "I'll just take this one for now though. Lainey wouldn't mind."

"Are you ready to go back then?" she asked.

"Got to," he said. "Need to get the ramp folded up and back here 'fore dawn."

Briar frowned. "All right."

"But you can come back here whenever you want," said Ferd. "Maybe if you don't mind sharing your secret spot with me?" He looked around the home. "It'd be awfully hard to find a new place like this."

"Yeah," she said. "That sounds good."

"All right then," said Ferd. "We best get back then. Moonlight's wasting."

Briar followed him out of his home and the culvert, the blue glow vanishing back to its boring, normal metal as he wandered out.

Ferd lay his hand on the ground again, opening his palm. "Care to ride again, m'lady?"

Briar chuckled as she stepped onto his palm. "Thank you, sir."

Ferd placed her in his pocket and turned back for the cemetery.

Briar hung on the pocket sleeve as Ferd strode through the woods, his footfalls and heat of his chest attempting to coax her back to sleep.

She slapped at her face to keep awake.

The moon dipped well past the midnight hour by the time they reached the cemetery again. From far away, Briar thought the wooden ramp against the ivy wall resembled one she built at home by laying a board down the stone steps.

"Oh, no," said Ferd as they drew nearer.

Briar stood taller in his pocket. "What's wrong?"

Ferd's shoulders sagged as he plucked her out and gently set her on the ground. "They're already gone," he said. "Look."

Briar followed his point and ran to the ramp, the grass beyond it trampled and pathways scattering in all directions towards the fields and woods.

"No way…" she said.

The rose-givers had left their marks upon the wood. Hoof prints and paw tracks, clawed scratches and tail brushings, tiny shoeprints or feet and toes no bigger than Trixie's all ran together up the ramp then muddied the path when they came back down.

Briar looked up at Ferd, her eyes gleaming. "They were here!"

"Yep," said Ferd. "And now they're gone again."

"I'm sorry, Ferd," said Briar. "Maybe next year we'll get in."

"You still can," he said. "Just got to go up that ramp."

Briar's gaze wandered up the wooden walkway. Then she looked on the flowerpot and dead rose Ferd had carried from his home. "No," she said. "I can wait too."

"Okay then." Ferd smiled. "Here."

He handed over the flowerpot then put his giant foot on the ramp.

"Stand back now," he said.

Briar backed up toward the woods as Ferd stepped his full weight onto the ramp and rocked.

"Ready?" he asked.

"I'm ready," she said.

"Here goes." Ferd took a deep breath and jumped. His landing sent a tremor up the ramp. It yielded like an unlocked door with hinges now swinging it free.

Ferd stepped off the wooden platform and the plywood pieces folded back into the others. Like a slinky finishing its journey to the bottom of a staircase, the last ramp piece fell, forming what seemed to be a single stack of plywood one would find in a lumberyard.

Briar giggled. "That is so cool."

"Yeah," said Ferd, taking the rope ends and tying them to keep the plywood pieces together. "Now I got to get it home 'fore dawn."

Briar kicked at the dirt. "Guess that means I need to go home too, huh?"

"I reckon so," said Ferd.

She felt his grubby fingers under her chin, bidding her look up into his big eyes.

"But I'll be down at the culvert," he said. "If you wanna come see me. Maybe bring me some of them, uh…"

"Epsom salts?" Briar asked.

Ferd nodded. "Yeah. Might be I could use them." He looked on his dead rose. "For next year."

Briar hugged on his finger. "I will."

He nudged her in the back with another. "Best get home now. I got to get moving on too."

"Okay." Briar stepped away. "Bye, Ferd. I'll see you soon."

He waved and then went to the ramp stack. Getting his fingers under it, he heaved and lifted the stack atop his shoulder, as if he lifted a straw bale. Then he headed for the woods.

Briar ran back to the tree where she'd left her bicycle and fetched it up by the handlebars. She swung her leg over the side, but didn't push off for home. She glanced back at the cemetery's ivy wall.

Then she looked up at the stars. *What's Mr. Coldwater and Jesse's uncle Ted gonna say this time, Grandpa?* She chuckled.

Briar heard a noise from inside the forest. She walked her bicycle closer to the tree, hiding, and peeked out.

Ferd had come back.

What's he looking for? she thought as she watched his head turn, surveying the area.

The big troll lumbered toward the ivy wall, kneeling beside it. His back blocked Briar's sight, but he stayed there a good while, his shoulders moving back and forth.

What's he doing? Briar wondered.

Ferd stood and rubbed a finger under his nose, then headed back for the woods, his footfalls quaking the earth beneath Briar.

She waited in the woods until the tremors stopped. Then she ran for the wall where he had kneeled. Briar slowed as she approached the trampled grass, her gaze training on what Ferd had busied himself with.

"Oh…" she uttered at seeing his wilted and moldy rose leaned against the wall and the loose dirt from where he had tried to plant it.

Briar felt wetness on her cheeks as she knelt beside the rose.

"Maybe next year." She tamped the dirt with her hand, knowing it didn't matter if there were air pockets or not since the rose was already dead, needing to do it anyway. "Maybe next year."

CHAPTER EIGHTEEN

The Believer

"Doyle, did you do this?" Daddy asked.

Briar leaned against the truck side, grinning, as she stared at the mound of roses on the grave of Lainey Grace.

"No, sir," said Doyle. "But I'll be danged if I can't hear ol' Bob laughing now, boy." He clapped Jesse on the shoulder. "Yessir. He'd be right tickled to see this mess. What you think?"

Jesse nodded. "Yeah, I guess he would."

Daddy shook his head. "Jesse, you didn't do this?"

"You think I wanna lose my job?" Jesse reached for his left breast pocket. He took out a toothpick and started chewing on the end. "No, sir. Uncle Ted's gonna have my hide when he comes in and sees this mess."

Doyle laughed. "Yeah, I expect you gonna have a good ol' time explaining this to him. Course I guess you could still blame Bob. Don't think he'd mind much now, do you, Russ?"

Daddy kicked at the grass. "Doggone it, Doyle. Knock it off. Now which one of you did this? 'Fess up."

"I know who it was, Daddy."

"Briar Ann, I ain't got time for your stories this morning."

They ain't stories. Briar slouched.

Daddy's face tightened, his gaze flitting from Doyle to Jesse and back again. "Which one of you did it?"

Doyle's face broke. "I don't know what to tell you, Russ. We ain't—"

"Stop it, Doyle." Daddy shouted. "Just stop it. You and Dad been playing these tricks forever now. It ain't funny no more. Not this year."

"Why, 'cause you think he's gone?" Doyle asked.

Briar thought Daddy's chin quivered.

"He is gone."

"Shoot," said Doyle. "He's right over there in space thirty-three if you need to have a talk with him." Doyle fixed his cap. "Matter of fact, I headed over there first thing this morning to have myself a little chat. Told him all about these roses. Might be that's just what you need."

"Doyle…"

"You know what, Russ." Doyle sidled up next to Briar, leaning against the truck, looking on the roses. "You're right. This ain't funny at all. You still think your daddy was just telling stories to pull your leg."

"I think you're still pulling it," said Daddy.

"Okay," said Doyle. "What you gonna say when I'm buried in here too and them roses show up?"

Daddy looked at Jesse.

"*Pssh,*" said Jesse. "Got me a roof over my head and a good job. You think I'm gonna risk all that to lay roses on some stranger's grave, you got another thing coming, hoss."

Daddy's fists clenched as he walked to the truck and climbed inside the cab.

"Where you going, Daddy?" Briar asked.

"Gotta get to work," he said, starting up the engine. "I'll see you at home, baby."

Briar and Doyle stepped toward Jesse as the truck drove away.

"He's mad," said Briar.

"Yes, ma'am, I expect he is," said Doyle. "He'll get over it."

Briar shot him a look.

"Yeah," said Doyle. "You might be right. Ain't like a Wade boy to give up on a grudge."

"Or a Wade girl." She tried to push him.

But Doyle laughed and danced away before she reached him.

Jesse took his toothpick out of his mouth. "What're we gonna do about these roses, Doyle?" He glanced toward the main entrance. "Won't be long 'til others find out and come on in here and we ain't got time to bag them all up."

"You tell me, boss," said Doyle. "It's your playbook we's following now."

Jesse turned and looked at Briar, his face masked in question.

"You wanted to see them again," she said, pointing at the roses, thinking on the wish Trixie granted her. "There they are."

Jesse nodded. "All right then."

"What then?" Doyle asked.

Jesse smirked. "We ain't gonna do nothing."

Briar cheered and ran to hug him.

"Well, hate to break up the party," said Doyle. "But I think someone else might have more to say on it."

Briar followed the jerk of his head toward a black, 1949 Hudson Commodore as it slowly drove up the cemetery drive.

Jesse whistled. "Whose car's that?"

"Mrs. Coldwater..." Briar stepped forward as the car parked.

The Coldwater manservant, Dmitri, stepped out of the car and opened the rear door.

Briar saw Mrs. Coldwater's hand shaking as she lifted a white hankie to her nose.

"Oh, my..." she said, her voice catching. "Dmitri, look. They...they're..."

"Beautiful, madam," said Dmitri, extending an open hand and helping her step away from the car.

Briar ran to her side, taking hold of her other arm. "Hello, Mrs. Coldwater."

"Oh, my dear," she said, patting Briar's hand. "You were right. They...they did come."

"Yes, ma'am, every year," said Briar. "When the last—"

"Leaf of summer falls," said Mrs. Coldwater, her body trembling as she leaned close to Briar and kissed her on the forehead. "Bless you, child."

Briar blushed. "But I didn't do nothing."

"You have," said Mrs. Coldwater, nodding. "You have."

A breeze swept up and Mrs. Coldwater closed her eyes, turning her face to the sun. She took a deep breath and exhaled slowly as the wind died down.

What's going on? Briar wondered, shivering.

"Dmitri." Mrs. Coldwater waved. "Dmitri, help me, please."

"Of course, madam," he said.

Briar stayed by Mrs. Coldwater's side too, the pair of them escorting the old woman toward the grave of Lainey Grace.

"Oh, they're beautiful," said Mrs. Coldwater. "Aren't they, dear? Have you ever seen such a thing in all your life, Dmitri? Have you ever seen so many roses?"

"Only here, madam," he said.

"D-Don't step on them," said Mrs. Coldwater, her fingers waving. "Please. Please, don't step on the roses."

"'Scuse us, ma'am—"

Briar glanced over her shoulder at Doyle and Jesse.

Doyle removed his hat, holding it over his chest. "We'll make you a path."

"Oh, thank you," said Mrs. Coldwater. "Thank you, my dears."

Briar left her side to help Doyle and Jesse, all three kneeling and gently picking up the roses, placing them on others. They cleared enough to make a walkway to the gravestone then Doyle and Jesse stepped back, bowing their heads as Briar and Dmitri aided Mrs. Coldwater up the mound.

The old woman collapsed by the gravestone, clinging to Briar's hand.

"Oh, my dear..." she kissed the stone then tore herself away, sobbing as she ran her fingers over the stone face. "Oh, my dear princess..."

"Princess?" Briar asked softly.

"Aye, all little girls are princesses, dear," said Mrs. Coldwater, her eyes shining as she turned back to the gravestone. "And she... she was mine. Her voice like a songbird, and her gown of white lace...you'll...you'll—"

Dmitri knelt beside her, picked up a red rose, and handed it to Mrs. Coldwater. "You will find no one kinder than the Princess Lainey Grace."

Briar kept silent as Mrs. Coldwater leaned to Dmitri and cried in his embrace. She glanced back at Doyle and Jesse and found both men's cheeks red and glistening in the morning sun.

"H-how did she live, ma'am?" Briar asked.

Mrs. Coldwater sniffled. "What was that, dear? How did she live?"

"Yes, ma'am," said Briar. "Grandpa Bob always said folks focus so much on how someone died that they forget to talk on how the person lived."

"Bless you, child." Mrs. Coldwater laughed through her tears. "Ah, but you are an old soul, aren't you?"

Briar nodded. "That's just what Grandpa Bob said about me too."

"Well, he was a wise man, wasn't he?" she asked. "And quite right as well. Eamon dwells so often on his grief that at times I find myself drowning in it too. All when we should remember our Lainey for the darling girl she was, full of hopes and... and life."

Mrs. Coldwater trembled and reached for Dmitri. "Oh, but she was lovely, wasn't she, Dmitri? My darling girl? And look... look! She has her roses."

"Lainey liked roses then?" Briar asked.

"Aye," said Mrs. Coldwater. "What girl does not? E-Eamon brought her fresh cut roses to the hospital every morning. Red roses, pink roses, d-different colors each day to surprise her." Mrs. Coldwater dabbed at her eyes. "A-after she died, w-we learned she'd been sneaking down the hall at night to give her roses to the other patients in the ward."

Mrs. Coldwater stopped to compose herself. She smiled at Briar. "The nurses said it always cheered the other children to wake up and find roses at their bedsides. That a mysterious stranger thought enough of them to leave something behind to brighten their morning." Mrs. Coldwater searched out Briar. "Do you know who brings these roses, dear?"

Briar sniffled and nodded. "I'm not supposed to—"

"Please," Mrs. Coldwater touched her arm. "Do tell me."

"You won't believe," said Briar.

"I will." Mrs. Coldwater nodded. "Oh, but of course I will. Everyone needs someone to believe in them. Please...who are they? Who brings the roses?"

"I've only met two," said Briar. "The first one was Trixie—"

"The leprechaun?" Mrs. Coldwater's voice caught in her throat.

Briar paled. "Do you know Ferd too?"

"Oh!" Mrs. Coldwater covered her mouth, her whole body shaking as she rocked in Dmitri's arms.

"Wh-what's wrong, ma'am?" Briar asked. "I didn't mean no—"

"They were her favorites," said Dmitri. "The rascal leprechaun and the gentle troll."

"They're mine too," said Briar to Mrs. Coldwater. "Did you meet them when you were a girl? Did Trixie trick wishes out of you?"

Mrs. Coldwater laughed. "He would have certainly tried, wouldn't he?" she said. "The little scoundrel."

Briar grinned as Mrs. Coldwater put the hankie to her nose and honked into it.

"H-How do you know of Trixie and Ferd, my dear?" Mrs. Coldwater asked.

"I met them," said Briar. "Here, near the cemetery. Trixie, he was caught in one of Doyle's ground squirrel traps and Ferd, well, he was outside the wall too, but can't get in on account of he's too big."

"Where are they now?" she asked. "Will you take me to them?"

Briar slumped. "I don't know where they went. Trixie comes and goes when he wants. And Ferd, he lives down by Newman Creek, underneath the culvert. I stole some Epsom salts out of the garage this morning for him. He keeps trying to grow this rose, but it dies every year. And then I rode my bike out there to give them salts to him, only..." Briar's eyes welled.

"What, dear?" Mrs. Coldwater asked. "What's wrong?"

"I couldn't find the door," she said. "It's closed up shut. And I don't know the song he hummed to make it open. But I left them Epsom salts, just in case he comes out when I'm not there."

Mrs. Coldwater smiled. "I'm certain he will be most pleased to find them and that you remembered him."

"Ma'am," said Briar. "Do you...how do you know about Ferd and Trixie?"

Mrs. Coldwater looked to the grave of Lainey Grace. "They were in her favorite book that we read from every night," Mrs. Coldwater touched the gravestone. "She was a lot like you. Feisty and curious, beautiful and with such imagination."

Briar licked her lips. "Ma'am, do you know why they bring the roses?"

"No," she said. "Do you?"

Briar shook her head. "They said it weren't their place to say. Not their story to tell."

Mrs. Coldwater reached for one of the red roses and brought it to her nose, smelling it. Then she looked on Briar. "Perhaps one day we'll find out together. Won't that be nice?"

"Yes, ma'am," said Briar. "It sure would."

"*It will be*," said Mrs. Coldwater, patting Briar's hands again. "Oh, but it certainly will be, my dear."

Year 12

CHAPTER NINETEEN

The Familiar Drive

"Think they'll come tonight, Little Miss?" Doyle asked as he yanked another dahlia out of the flowerbed.

Briar shielded her eyes and searched out all the trees within sight. She grinned at not finding a single leaf among them. "Maybe," she said. "Just maybe. Weather's right for it."

Doyle licked his thumb, dirt and all, and put it to the wind. "Why, yep. I think you might just be right."

Briar took the dahlia he'd uprooted and pruned its tubers down to the bulbs. Then she laid them inside the apple crate box she had rescued from Grandpa Bob's apartment.

"Well." Doyle stood, surveying their work. "I think this right here would do ol' Bob proud."

Briar looked on their haul—nearly twenty bulbs rescued for the next spring. "Yep," she said. "I think so."

"You gonna stay here and finish up then?" he asked.

"Yessir," she said. "I'll be along after a while. You can tell Jesse I'll be out before he needs to lock up."

"All right then," said Doyle. "You take care now. I'll see you and them roses here tomorrow. Give my regards to Mrs. Coldwater."

Briar waved then returned to her pruning shears.

The wind kicked up and Briar sat back on her heels, closing her eyes, embracing its chill to cool her from the sweat of hard work. When she opened them again, a single rose lay in front of her, its petals shimmering green with gold tips.

"Trixie…"

Briar fetched up the rose and glanced all around the cemetery, swearing she heard the leprechaun's laughter.

"Trixie," she called. "Does this mean you and the others are coming tonight?"

The leprechaun laughed again, this time behind her.

Briar spun, again seeing nothing. "Do I get my third wish tonight?"

"Aye," Trixie called out, his voice surrounding her. "But take care, and see it used ere the dawn. For it's your last wish from this leprechaun."

Briar stood. "Show yourself!"

But Trixie said nothing in reply.

"Gone again…" Briar sneered. "Stupid leprechauns."

Briar looked on the rose, twirling it between her fingers, the green and gold colors mixing together the faster she spun it. She laughed and placed the rose inside the apple crate. Then she picked up the crate and ran for the main gate.

Doyle had already taken off for home by the time Briar

reached the groundskeeper office. She found the office door unlocked and dropped off the crate inside. She grabbed the rose and twirled it again.

I need to tell someone!

She skipped about the office then ran back outside to pick up her bicycle. Then she put the rose upside down in the tin bucket wired to the handlebars to not lose its petals as she rode.

Briar glanced toward the cemetery and wheeled her bicycle around, headed back inside. She pedaled hard toward the Coldwater's private gate, waving at Jesse on the riding lawnmower as he cut the lawn in the Catholic section.

"They're coming tonight!" she yelled at him. "Jesse!"

But he only pointed to his ears, shook his head, and kept mowing.

Briar continued on anyway. She flew under the archway and blew kisses at the gargoyles as she rode up the familiar private drive.

The wind swept in front of her, whirling the leaves in a tornado of autumn delight.

Briar pedaled through it, the leaves slapping at her face. She laughed through it all, her legs pumping to reach the mansion and share the news with Mrs. Coldwater and Dmitri.

The fountain spewed geysers from the mouths of the selkies and mermaids, the waters green and clear.

Briar leaned hard to the left on her bicycle, dipping it low as she dared not spill it, and rounded the fountain. She spun to quick stop, careful not to leave a skid mark.

She swung off and leaned the bicycle against the fountain, then ran for the door. "Mrs. Coldwater!" Briar rapped the lion knockers. "Dmitri! They're coming tonight. The rose-givers are—"

The door creaked open halfway, a scowling Mr. Coldwater behind it.

Briar backed off the stoop. "Wh-where is Mrs. Coldwater?"

"She won't be receiving any callers today," he said.

"But...why?" Briar asked. "The rose—"

"Dmitri," said Mr. Coldwater. "Dmitri, come here at once!"

Briar glanced up to the second floor and the white lace curtains where she and Mrs. Coldwater often sat for tea and biscuits. "What's going on?" she asked Mr. Coldwater. "Where is she?"

Dmitri appeared at the door. "You called, sir?"

Mr. Coldwater nodded and pointed his silver cane at Briar. "See this child home," he said. "Tell her parents she is not allowed back."

Dmitri's eyes lingered on Briar. "Sir, if I may—"

"You may not," said Mr. Coldwater. "See her home, or see yourself gone with her."

Dmitri nodded. "Yes, sir."

Briar stepped forward. "But, she wanted to know. She asked me to—"

Mr. Coldwater stamped his cane end on the ground then staggered out into the drive. "My wife is sick and dying," he said. "She has appreciated your visits over this past year, as I am sure you are most aware, but we have no need of unwanted company at this time. Good day."

"But I'm not unwanted—"

The door slammed.

Briar walked back to her bicycle, then looked up to the window again. "Mrs. Coldwater! They're coming tonight!"

The door reopened and Dmitri hurrying out of it. "Be quiet," he shushed.

Briar swung her leg over the bicycle.

Dmitri was faster and caught her around the waist.

"Let me go!" Briar shouted.

"Listen to me," he said.

"I won't," she struggled against him, though it mattered little against his strength.

"Please, for Mrs. Coldwater," he said. *"And for Lainey Grace."*

Briar stopped fighting. "Wh-what do you mean?"

Dmitri set her feet back to the ground. "Come, Miss Briar," he said, waving her follow him toward the garage.

Briar didn't move. "Tell me why first."

"Not here," said Dmitri. "Too many eyes watching. Too many ears listening."

Briar followed his nod to the mansion. One of the curtains fluttered. *Mr. Coldwater?*

Dmitri opened one of the garage doors to a host of vintage automobiles.

She wheeled her bicycle after him.

Dmitri chose a '51 Chevy with sleek black paint and opened the door. "Allow me to drive you home now, Miss," he said.

"No," she said. "You tell me—"

"Come with me—" Dmitri leaned close, whispering, "And I will pass on whatever secrets you would have Mrs. Coldwater know."

Briar took the rose out of the tin bucket then turned over her bicycle to Dmitri. She hopped in the truck and shut the door. *Grandpa Bob would have loved this,* she thought, settling into the leather seat with Trixie's rose in her lap.

Dmitri climbed in and started the engine, then eased out of the garage.

"So what's wrong with her?" Briar asked.

"Her body tires of this world," he said, "her spirit eager to leave it and rejoin her daughter."

Briar turned silent as they drove the private drive. She saw the Coldwater gate approaching and fought off the pit in her stomach. "But she can't die. Not now. Not yet. We've been waiting all year for the fall."

"Death waits for no one," said Dmitri as the truck passed under the gargoyle archway. "I know she wants to see the secret givers, but—"

"Good. They're coming tonight. See," She lifted the rose. "Trixie left this for me so I would know. I have to use my third wish."

Dmitri smiled. "I will tell her for you, but I fear your friends come too late. She is weak now," he said. "Very weak. She has not left her bed in three days now."

"Will you take her this?" Briar offered him the rose. "Tell her for me?"

"Aye." Dmitri took the rose and tucked its stem into his kerchief pocket. "She will be pleased to see it, no doubt. But do not allow your hopes to rise."

"Thank you," said Briar.

Dmitri nodded.

They drove out of the cemetery and Briar waved to Jesse in the office as they passed. She sighed and turned to Dmitri, staring on his pale skin and slicked back hair, thinking on his hard accent that sent chills down her spine. "Can I ask you something?"

"Anything, Miss," he said.

"Are you one of them?"

His eyebrow raised. "What do you think?"

"I dunno," she said. "Just had to ask."

"Ah, but what would I be? I am no troll or leprechaun—"

"Vampire," she said. "Definitely."

Dmitri chuckled. "It is said vampires cannot walk in daylight."

"Then what are you?" Briar asked.

"*Half*-vampire." He grinned.

Briar laughed, seeing Dmitri had no fangs, still uncertain if he was kidding her or not.

CHAPTER TWENTY

The Fire Between

Daddy waited on the porch as they turned in the drive.

Briar's gut pained as he approached the truck, his face masked in sternness.

"Evening," said Daddy to Dmitri. "Thanks for bringing her home and not taking her straight down to the station."

"Daddy, I—"

"Get out of the truck, Briar," said Daddy calmly, opening the door for her.

Briar swallowed the lump in her throat. She gave Dmitri a last look, then climbed out.

Daddy lifted her bicycle out of the back, but kept hold of the handlebars so Briar couldn't take it. Then he looked back inside the truck at Dmitri. "You tell Mr. Coldwater this won't happen again. I mean to make sure of it. I already told him on the phone, but I'd like him to hear another time, if you don't mind."

"I will tell him," said Dmitri.

"Thanks," said Daddy, closing the door.

Briar fled to the porch as Dmitri backed out of the drive and onto the road.

Daddy waited until the Coldwater manservant was gone then took out his pocketknife and flicked open the blade.

"Daddy," said Briar. "Wh-what are you doing?"

Her heart leapt to her throat as he spun the handle in his palm and punctured her bicycle's front wheel.

"*Daddy, no!*"

"I told you," he said, wiggling the blade free and stabbing the rear wheel, "not to go up there."

"Daddy, why…" Briar collapsed on the steps, sobbing, as he flung the bicycle into the yard.

"You know why," he said. "Get in the house."

Briar shook her head, her mouth opening and shutting wordlessly.

Daddy grabbed her by the arm and led her up the steps. "When I tell you to do something, you do it."

"Daddy—"

He threw open the screen door and carried her inside. "How many times I got to tell you something before you listen?"

"My bike…"

"I don't care about your bike," he said. "I told you—"

"Grandpa gave that to me," she said.

"Yeah? Whattaya think he would've done if you hadn't listened to him either, huh?"

Briar trembled. "He wouldn't have…he would have believed me." She shook her head. "I just wanted to tell her—"

"I don't care what you wanted," said Daddy. "You ain't never going up there again. And I got news for you, Little Miss. You ain't going back into the cemetery either. I'm done hearing about them roses."

Briar's face paled.

"You sulk all you want." Daddy pointed down the hall. "But you do it in your room. You're grounded."

"The rose-givers—"

She winced when Daddy raised his hand.

The slap didn't fall—his hand hung in the air, caught, it seemed to Briar, by something invisible.

"Daddy..." she said. "I'm sorry."

Momma appeared in the kitchen entry. "What's going on in here?"

His shoulders shaking, Daddy dropped his hand to his side and backed against the door. His chin dropped to his chest and there were tears in his eyes when he looked up at her.

"Get in your room, Briar Ann," he said, his voice quivering. "Don't come back out 'til I say."

Briar fled down the hall to her room, diving into her bed the moment after she shut the door. She wept into her pillows then screamed her anger at Mr. Coldwater for not listening and at Daddy for not believing her.

She felt her bedding dip and turned to see Momma seated beside her. Briar sat up and buried her head into Momma's shoulder, sobbing.

Momma stroked her hair, shushing her. "It's all right, baby. You're all right."

"Wh-why did he do that, Momma?"

"You're growing up now," she said. "It's time you started listening."

"He—he cut my tires," said Briar. "He looked like he wanted to hit me."

"Briar, you look at me now."

Briar choked on her tears as Momma leaned back.

"Your daddy loves you more than anything in this world," said Momma. "And he's out there right now beating himself up for what he just did."

"He should be," said Briar.

Momma's lips pursed. "He's trying, baby. We're all trying. But even mommas and daddies make mistakes."

Briar glanced up at the ceiling and the two dried roses hung above her bed. *I know what's real,* she thought, looking back at Momma. "Grandpa Bob didn't make mistakes."

"He did," said Momma. "And he'd tell you that too if he were here right now."

"I don't believe that," said Briar. "You tell me one mistake he ever made."

Momma sighed. "The first time your grandpa ever told your daddy he loved him was that day in the hospital, right before he died."

Briar wiped her cheeks. "What?"

"Your daddy didn't hear that growing up," said Momma. "Oh, it didn't mean that Grandpa Bob didn't love him. He just didn't know how to say it. Men are funny like that. They get so caught up with the idea of being strong for everyone else, they don't always remember those few little words are all the strength we need."

"But Grandpa Bob told me all the time," said Briar.

Momma nodded. "That's because he looked back on his life

and wanted to do better. He was trying, baby. We're all trying, just like we all make mistakes sometimes. It's part of life. One day you'll be a momma and you'll make mistakes too."

Briar looked out her window at her bicycle in the yard, the rubber ripped and torn. "I wouldn't ever do that."

"No, probably not," said Momma. "Because you'll remember it and want to do better. Just like your daddy is trying to do."

"He's not trying," she said.

"Briar Ann," said Momma. "When was the last time you heard your daddy say I love you?"

Briar shrugged. "Last night."

"Mmm-hmm," said Momma. "And the night before that and every night since you were born. He loves you more than he knows how to say, Little Miss. And as upset as you are right now, believe me when I tell you that your daddy will be kicking himself for this far longer than you will."

"Huh uh," said Briar. "I won't ever forget."

"Briar," said Momma. "He did wrong with that bicycle, and he knows it, but I'm not going to sit here and listen to you talk poor on him. Your daddy's a good man and you're lucky to have him. Some might look and sound a little smoother around the edges, but yours would do anything for you. One of these days you're gonna realize you couldn't have had a better one."

Momma got up from the bed and left the room.

Briar glanced at the bedside clock and the picture she'd stolen off Grandpa Bob's fridge of Daddy and his first car.

6:30 p.m.

Then she buried her face in the pillows again, crying herself to sleep.

She woke to a soft rapping on her door and glanced at the bedside clock. *10:00 p.m.*

"Baby," said Daddy's voice, quietly from the opposite side. "Briar, can I come in?"

"Go away," she said.

"I ain't going nowhere," he said. "Not 'til I get to talk with you. I'll stay out here all night if I have to."

Fine, Briar thought.

"I'm sorry," he said. "I'm sorry, Briar."

She stormed out of bed and flung open the door.

Daddy stood in the same clothes he had on when she came home. His hair was tussled like he'd run his hands through it a thousand times over and his cheeks were still red from crying.

"Hi," he said.

"What do you want?"

"Just to talk with you," he said. "Get your coat. We're going somewhere."

Briar blinked. "Now?"

Daddy nodded. "Meet me out front. I already got the truck running and the heat going." He wiped his nose. "I'll see you out there."

Briar watched him go. *What's gotten into him?*

She ran to fetch her Carhartt jacket off the bed. Throwing it on, she ran down the hall and saw the front door open.

Momma was waiting by the entry with a mug of steaming coffee.

"Momma," said Briar. "What's going on with Daddy?"

"I told you he's trying, baby." She hugged Briar, kissing her on the head. "Don't keep him out too late. Go on now. He's waiting on you."

Briar pushed open the screen door.

Daddy was already in the truck, the tailpipe spitting white exhaust that Briar thought looked like a ghost flying for heaven.

She ran through it, the diesel scent filling her nose, and found Daddy had leaned across the seat to shove open her door.

Briar climbed inside.

"You ready?" he asked.

Briar buckled her seatbelt. "Where we going?"

"The cemetery." Daddy threw the truck in gear. "I hear them rose-givers are coming tonight."

CHAPTER TWENTY-ONE

Third Wish

Daddy turned the vents toward Briar as he pulled out of their drive.

"Daddy," she said. "Why we doing this?"

"Got to thinking about what you said about me not believing you and all. Been chewing on it quite a bit." He shook his head. "Made me remember Dad and that Chevelle of mine."

"A car?" Briar asked.

Daddy nodded. "We saw one up at the state fair once when I was a kid. Thought it was the most beautiful thing I'd ever seen, so I told Dad I was gonna get me one someday." Daddy clicked his teeth. "Course he didn't believe me...not 'til I drove one right up to the groundskeeper office, that is. Same day he snapped that picture of me that you took off his fridge."

"He told me it was a good day," said Briar. "What'd Grandpa say when he saw your car for the first time?"

"Asked me who I stole it off of."

Briar laughed as Daddy grinned, showing off the dimples Grandpa Bob passed onto him.

"He couldn't doubt me after that though," said Daddy. "Point is, it weren't just about having that car. I was showing him he was wrong to doubt me." Daddy sighed. "Yeah, and that I needed him to know it."

Daddy reached over the seat, rubbing her shoulder.

"I don't want that fire between us, Little Miss," he said. "Don't want you thinking I ain't got no belief in you and that you got to prove yourself. Sometimes even daddies got to remember that just 'cause they ain't seen it yet, don't mean it ain't possible."

Briar blushed. "Yeah?"

"Yes, ma'am," he said. "I know Dad believed in them rose-givers, even if he didn't figure their secret out. Other times, I wonder if he did, only knew it'd prove me wrong after all these years of naysaying him and Doyle."

"They didn't find out their secrets, Daddy," said Briar.

"I believe that," he said. "Dad might've kept his mouth shut for me to save face, but Doyle sure wouldn't."

Briar laughed.

"So," said Daddy. "Where are we headed to meet these rose givers?"

"Out in the woods."

Daddy tapped his fingers against the steering wheel. "Thought you wanted to get inside the cemetery."

"I do," said Briar.

"You call a fire engine truck to come out and meet us with a ladder?"

"Nope," she said. "I got something better than that. I got a Ferd."

"A what?"

Briar grinned. "You'll see. Just head for the culvert near Newman Creek and pull over to the side of the road when we get to the woods."

"All right," said Daddy, his tone doubting.

Briar patted her hands against the dashboard as they passed the cemetery.

The main gates were locked, but Jesse's light was on in the living room of Grandpa Bob's former house.

Sorry, Jesse, she thought. *Maybe next year we'll stop to get you too.*

Daddy sped on past. "You sure about this? Ol' Jess seems to have turned over a new leaf this past year. Might be we could talk him into allowing us inside the cemetery tonight."

Briar fixed a stare on him. "You believe me or not?"

They kept going.

"Here," said Briar, once they had driven a ways down the dirt road. "Turn in here."

The brakes squealed as Daddy drove off half in the grass and slowed.

Briar hopped out before Daddy had the truck in park. She blew her breath on the chill wind and looked up at the half moon. "Come on," she yelled. "We gotta hurry or else them and Ferd might already be gone."

"Who's Ferd?"

Briar didn't bother answering. She ran around the truck and grabbed Daddy by the hand then led deeper into the woods. Through bramble and brush, their feet stomped over the dead leaves, but always Briar kept the cemetery wall within her sights, looking ahead for any sight of Ferd.

"There!" she said, seeing the ramp already in place. "Daddy, do you see it?"

Daddy stopped. "What the..."

"I told you," she said. "I told you it was real."

Daddy tugged on her hand. "Come on. W-We need to go back to the truck. Call Jesse maybe."

"No," said Briar. "We're not calling him. My friend, Ferd, will be waiting for us up ahead. I just know it."

"Briar, who's Ferd?"

She shrugged. "He's a troll."

Then she let go of Daddy's hand and ran for the ramp.

"Briar Ann, wait!"

"Ferd," Briar yelled before reaching the clearing. "Ferd, I'm here. I made it!" She stopped shy of the ramp when the glum troll didn't appear. "Ferd?"

Daddy clomped behind her, trying to catch his breath. "How did this...how did this get here?"

"Oh, shoot." Briar kicked the ramp. "He probably forgot his rose again and had to go home for it."

Daddy bent over, sucking air, then put his hands atop his head. He backed up on the ramp at the sight of all the trampled grass. "What happened here?"

Briar glanced up the ramp way. "Look," she said, pointing to the prints and tracks leading up. "Some of them are already inside."

She sprinted for the top.

"Briar..." Daddy called. "Come back, honey. It's not safe."

Briar ran all the way, not pausing until she stood atop the wall.

"Baby, come on now," said Daddy. "I believe you there's someone in there. But let's go talk to Jesse and we'll walk in."

Briar hesitated, glancing toward the woods, torn between waiting on Ferd and descending the ramp into the cemetery.

Something rustled near her foot.

Briar glanced down. "Trixie?"

The leprechaun climbed out of the ivy and gave her a little bow. "My, look at us, all perched here on the wall. What should happen, ye think, if we were to fall?"

"Don't," said Briar, turning to better keep him in her sight. "I'm not like you. I can't fly down."

Trixie waved off her concerns. "Ah, ye don't weigh much, you're just a wee lass." He peeked over the side. "It won't hurt too bad, if ye fall in the grass."

"Briar," said Daddy, walking up the ramp. "Who are you talking to, baby? Come back down before you fall."

"You stay there, Trixie." Briar warned. "I promised Ferd I wouldn't go in without—" She straightened. "That's it…my third wish. I could use it to wish for Ferd to go in. Trixie—"

The leprechaun grinned. "You've almost got it. Just need a wee last push!"

Trixie jumped at Briar, shoving her backwards.

She rolled down the ramp, the ivy wall and stars above mixing as one with Trixie's laughter in her ears.

"Oh, by the way, lass. Try to land on your tush!"

The ramp dumped her onto the grass and she kept rolling until her arms and legs fell flat.

Briar groaned.

"What's that?" someone whispered.

"Oh, look she's here!"

"Is it her?"

Briar sat up, her mind dizzy as she searched out the voices. "H-Hello," she said, glancing at the headstones, seeing the moonlight reflect off them. "Who's there?"

Then she saw them no reflections at all.

"Come on," said a voice. "Let's go see her. It's just the wee lass."

"Oh, no! How did she fall?"

"But her father—"

"He can't see us from up on the wall."

Briar gasped as gophers and moles waddled around the gravestones toward her. A few of them stood up on their hind legs, removing their hoods and staring at her.

"Are you…you're leprechauns too," said Briar.

Trixie bounded past her, cackling. "Aye, these are my mates, lass, and that one's a brownie." He pointed at one in a gopher skin. "Aye, Grumpkin's his name, all mopey and frownie."

The gopher-skinned little man folded his arms while the others laughed high-pitched giggles.

"Briar!" Daddy ran down the ramp. "Honey, are you okay?"

The leprechauns and brownies scattered, donning their animal camouflage, fleeing to hide behind the headstones.

Daddy reached the ramp's end and pulled Briar close. "I thought I lost you," he said. "You scared—"

"Daddy, look," said Briar, pointing throughout the cemetery.

Creatures of all different sizes and shapes drew nearer, some walking on two legs and others four. Some not walking at all.

Fairies flew with a trail of glitter in their wake, and Briar stepped aside to avoid it. Fauns and satyrs danced toward her while bare-chested centaurs and minotaurs strode regally over.

There were unicorns and talking beasts who whispered and nodded as they cast furtive glances at her. Werewolves blinked at her with golden eyes, their tongues lagging out of their mouths as they panted.

And whether in their mouths, hands, claws, or tails, all carried roses.

Briar cried at the sight of so many creatures smiling at her.

"What's wrong, baby?" Daddy asked.

"Can't you see them?" she asked.

Daddy put the back of his hand to her forehead. "I think the cemetery's playing games with you. Or else it's that tumble you took."

Briar glanced around the circle of creatures that surrounded them, watchful and whispering. "How can you not see them?" Briar asked.

"See who?"

Briar opened her mouth, but stopped short seeing Trixie wave at her.

He lifted his hand and flicked three fingers in the air. Then he winked and rubbed his hands together.

Briar grinned. "Trixie," she said. "I wish my daddy and everyone else could see all of you...*tonight*."

Trixie's face turned red and his ears wiggled back and forth. Then he thumbed his nose at her. "*Granted*."

Then he took off, laughing.

"Oh!" Daddy said, backing toward the ramp.

"What?" she asked. "Do you—"

"I see them, baby," he said, his eyes wide, head spinning. "I see them all."

"Come with us," said the brownie, Grumpkin. "We'll lead you! There's more to see!"

Briar grabbed Daddy's hand and ran further into the cemetery, following the other creatures as more beings paced beside them. Briar lost track of where they led her, trying to listen in on all their conversations.

She didn't look up until they turned silent.

The Coldwater's private entrance lay before her, its gates locked.

Briar stepped toward the bars, glancing up at the stone gargoyles.

Then they moved.

"Whoa…" Briar stepped back.

The gargoyles smiled and flexed their claws, loosing themselves of their holds, then flew down to join her and the others. One of them brushed her in the back with its wing, nudging her toward the gates.

Trixie jumped in front of her, bowing.

"And now I make good, lass, you who set me free, if ye recall your first wish, I owe a silver key." Trixie delved into his pocket and produced a gate key, handing it over.

Briar took the key. "Where did you get this?"

Trixie's eyes flashed. "Found it in the pocket of some gent named Ted, but this key liked it better in Trixie's instead."

The leprechaun urged her forward.

"Go on then, lass, and unlock these gates. At the end of this drive…someone awaits."

Briar put the key in the lock, and turned it until hearing the click. She took hold of the wrought iron bars and tugged it open.

Daddy joined her on the other side, taking the opposite gate. "You ready?"

Briar nodded and, together, they walked the gates back to the iron stakes. Briar knelt to the wire and slipped it over the end, ensuring the gates wouldn't swing closed again.

Far up the private drive, a pair of headlights flicked on, blinding her.

Briar lifted her arm to shield her eyes.

The creatures gasped as the headlights drove steadily onward, approaching them in the cemetery.

Briar stepped over to Daddy, clutching at his hand about her shoulder.

The Coldwater's black, 1949 Hudson Commodore rolled under the archway, and came to a halt. Dmitri slid out of the car and opened the rear door.

Briar found Mr. Coldwater's eyes wide and his mouth open as he took Dmitri's hand and climbed out, the bottom of his silver cane shaking before it found the ground to steady itself.

"It's not…it's not possible," Mr. Coldwater said, his eyes shining. Then he laughed and turned back to the car, rapping on the window. "Dear, look! Look! It's Unkett and Tristl." He pointed his cane into the crowd. "Oh, and there's Cant-Soo…and… and—Oh!"

Mr. Coldwater collapsed into a centaur's arms. "Talisien," he said. "My oldest friend. H-how are you here?"

"Sir," said the roan-backed centaur, his voice deep and weighty. "Would you allow another old friend the honor of carrying you and your wife? There is much and more for you both to see this night."

"Wh-why, yes." Mr. Coldwater turned back to the car, his eyes glazing over. "Dear? Would that be all right?"

Dmitri aided Mrs. Coldwater out of her car, her skin near pale as the white robe she clutched around her. She looked on the creatures with her sparkling blue eyes and gasped. "Oh, my…"

A gale forced Briar and the others away from the car.

Briar looked up and gasped, clutching Daddy's hand tighter as a winged lion descended. He shook his tawny mane and padded toward the Coldwaters.

"Agreyel," said Mr. Coldwater, shuffling toward the lion, his hand outstretched. "Is it really you?"

The winged lion yawned then nuzzled its head against him, nearly knocking the old man over.

Mr. Coldwater buried his face in its mane. "It *is* you." He turned to Mrs. Coldwater, laughing with tears in his eyes. "Dear, it's Agreyel. It's him!"

"I see," she said, leaning on Dmitri's arm.

Briar wiped her eyes as the winged lion lay its belly to the ground and she giggled when Mr. Coldwater hurried to climb on its back.

"Come on, dear," he said. "Come on."

Briar and Daddy laughed with the crowd of creatures as Mr. Coldwater bounced on the winged lion's back.

"Oh, do stop that at once, Eamon," said Mrs. Coldwater as Dmitri sat her behind Mr. Coldwater. She clutched tighter to her husband's chest. "Don't want me to fall off, do you?"

"Apologies, dear," he said. "But I'm on a winged lion!"

Briar giggled at his enthusiasm and she stepped back with all the others when Agreyel flapped his massive wings, kicking up dust.

"Oh!" she said, scooting closer to Daddy as Agreyel rose from the ground and flew above them.

He gave another flap of his wings, and turned to the east, flying away with Mr. Coldwater's mad laughter echoing all the way.

"Come," said the centaur to the crowd. "Lainey Grace awaits."

Briar leaned close to Daddy. "Do we follow them?" she whispered as the other creatures and beings turned to go.

"I don't know," he said. "I suppose so."

Briar felt a tug on her pants and glanced down to see Trixie's mischievous face. "What?" she asked.

"It's not my concern, really, but ye do have that key. So tell me, dear Briar, is there nowhere else to be?"

"No," she said. "Not that I can—"

"Kind of ye to let them in. Aye, your right to decide." Trixie jerked his head toward the Coldwater's private entrance. "Ye opened this gate, but there's still others outside."

"Trixie, what do you—" Briar's eyes widened. "Ferd!"

CHAPTER TWENTY-TWO

A Spot of Color

Briar abandoned the Coldwater's private gate and ran toward the public gateway with Daddy by her side. "Ferd!" she cried. "Ferd, I'm coming!"

"Briar," said Daddy. "Keep your voice down. You'll wake Jesse."

Briar's heart thudded against her chest as she sighted the main gate's archway. She rounded the corner drive and stopped short.

He was all alone, standing outside the locked main entry gates, his big face pressed against the wrought iron bars, and he stood on his tiptoes as if it might help him better see further in.

"Helloooo," he called. "Is anyone in there?"

"Oh, Ferd," Briar's voice was hushed at seeing he cradled a potted vase in hand. It had a plastic bag over the top and a bit of twine tied in a bow.

"Helloooo," said Ferd. "I need someone to take my rose, please. I finally got one worth giving."

Daddy rubbed Briar's back. "Is that your friend?"

Briar nodded and ran toward the gate. "Ferd! I'm here, Ferd!"

The big troll bonked his nose on the iron gates as he jerked away, frighted by her voice. "Oh," he said, seeing her. "It's you."

Briar reached the gates and stared up at him. "It's me."

Ferd grinned. "I thought you forgot about me like all the rest."

"I didn't," she said, fumbling for the silver gate key. "I wouldn't forget you."

Her hand shook as she reached through the bars and fit the key into the lock. She gave it a turn and heard it click. She didn't bother waiting on Daddy, pushing the gate open enough to run around it. Briar threw herself at Ferd, hugging on his leg, sobbing.

"Hi, Ferd," she said.

"Hi," he drawled.

Briar looked up into his doe-brown eyes. Then she glanced back at the cemetery. "You—" her voice caught. "You wanna come inside with the others?"

"Really?" he asked, his eyes welling.

"Yeah," she said, grabbing hold of the gate and swinging it wide, snaring the wire over the stake to keep it open. Then she ran to the other gate and opened it too. "Come on, Ferd."

Ferd looked around as he staggered forward, concern washing over his face. He glanced back at the woods then looked on Briar. "I-I don't know…"

"Come on," she said. "You can. Everyone else is waiting at the grave of Lainey Grace for us."

"O-okay." Ferd stepped to the gates and bent low to not strike his head upon the archway. He stood up on the other side, his big belly shaking as he chuckled. "I...I never thought I'd make it in here."

"You are now," said Briar. "Come on. Let's go."

"W-wait," he said.

"Why?"

Ferd pointed out the gates, toward the woods. "I'm not the only one who's been waiting."

Briar turned and gasped. *Giants!*

She saw cyclops and orcs, sasquatch and ogres—all the creatures too heavy to climb up Ferd's ramp now crossed the road in twos and threes, carrying roses dwarfed by the size of their fists. The ground shook as they tread closer and passed through the gates.

Briar heard someone scream.

"Jesse," Daddy yelled, running toward the house to quiet him. "Jesse, it's all right."

Briar stayed with Ferd as the creatures carried on by.

Daddy returned with Jesse, his face pale.

Briar laughed. "You wanted to see the roses."

Jesse gulped and leaned on Daddy.

"Can we go now?" Ferd asked. "I think that's all of us."

"Yeah," said Briar. "Let's go."

She led the way with Ferd lumbering at her side, his gait uneven and pitched, while Daddy and Jesse followed close behind.

The horde of creatures cleared a path for them as they neared the grave of Lainey Grace, the lot of them bowing away, others nodding to Briar. None spoke a word.

Briar's throat felt dry as they approached the mound.

Mr. and Mrs. Coldwater sat together at the grave, the thousands of roses surrounding them.

Briar thought the roses like a floral gateway as none of the others creatures dared cross the boundary.

Ferd stopped where the roses began. "Here," he said to Briar, handing her the vase he carried. He tucked his patchwork shirt into the burlap pants and tied his belt rope tighter to ensure they stayed up. Then he got down on one knee.

"Ferd," Briar asked as he took back the vase. "What are you doing?"

"You'll see," he whispered.

Then he leaned over the roses, nudging a few of them aside enough to put his palm on the ground.

What's he doing? Briar wondered.

Ferd leaned further still and tapped Mrs. Coldwater on the shoulder. "Ma'am."

Mrs. Coldwater turned, her face bunching up at the sight of him. "Ferd..."

"Yes, ma'am," he said.

Mrs. Coldwater reached for her husband. "Eamon...Eamon, look, it's him. He's here too."

"Ferd?" Mr. Coldwater asked, his body trembling. "Oh my. Wh-where have you been, you old troll?"

"Couldn't get in, sir," said Ferd. "Someone done locked up them gates every year. But Miss Briar let me in."

Briar grinned.

"Did she?" Mr. Coldwater wiped his eyes. "Well, I...I...I'm sorry, Ferd. Had I known you were out there—"

"It's okay," said Ferd. "I got in now. Brought something too. Been waiting a long time for this."

He leaned back and motioned for Briar to give him the

plastic-wrapped vase. Taking it in hand, he turned again to the husband and wife, offering it to Mr. Coldwater.

"Wh-what's this?"

"It's for you," said Ferd.

"A gift for me?" Mr. Coldwater asked. "But why?"

Ferd nodded. "Open it and see."

Briar tread a path through the roses, careful not to squish them, as Mr. Coldwater unwrapped the twine and then removed the plastic.

"Oh..." Briar gasped with the crowd at seeing the blue rose, its petal ends tipped violet.

Mr. Coldwater looked at his wife then touched the rose. "It's beautiful, Ferd. Sh-she would have loved it."

"She does," said Ferd. "Knew you would too. That's why she asked me to bring it to you."

Briar glanced at Ferd. *She's alive?*

"What did you say?" Mr. Coldwater asked.

"It's for you," said Ferd. "They're all for you. All of the roses."

"B-but why?" asked Mr. Coldwater, his gaze wandering over the faces in the crowd and the teeming piles of roses. "Why for me?"

"When all the leaves are falling and the land's turning brown and cold"—Ferd nodded to the blue rose—"Thought you could do with a spot of color. Remind you that everything's not dead and dying in the world. Why do you think we wait 'til the last leaf of summer falls?"

"I-I don't know, Ferd."

"Nothing but boring brown everywhere you look." Ferd grinned. "'Cept for these roses."

Mr. Coldwater chuckled as he looked on the blue rose. "You're right, Ferd. I-I have been shut away all this time." Mr. Coldwater looked on the faces of all those in the crowd. "And I have neglected all of you as well, haven't I?"

Ferd nodded. "That's why she sent us, another reminder for you to get to. She needs to know how the story ends."

"So do I, my dear troll." Mr. Coldwater laughed. "So do I. Why, I've not written a word about any of you since she passed. Though you have all ever been in my mind, I assure you."

Briar started forward. "What story, sir?"

Mr. Coldwater wiped his eyes. "The one I wrote for my sweet little girl as she lay in that nasty hospital ward." He touched the grave of Lainey Grace. "*The Ainslian Tales*...something to believe in. I-I wanted to give her a break from the harshness of it all."

Briar glanced up as Daddy hugged on her.

Mr. Coldwater pointed to the crowd. "Y-You lot helped me give her that for a time, didn't you?"

Briar searched the faces of the creatures, watching them nod and whisper to each other.

Mr. Coldwater lifted the blue rose vase then nodded his head to other roses. "Perhaps these will help me sort you out. I swear to not abandon you again."

Mrs. Coldwater took her husband's hand and squeezed it. "Thank you, Ferd," she said. "Thank you all."

Briar felt Daddy kiss her forehead, his lips lingering. "I love you, Little Miss," he whispered. "Love you more every day."

"I love you too, Daddy." Briar hugged him back as the creatures squeezed around them to approach the Coldwaters.

Jesse pushed in next to Briar and Daddy, his neck turning

every which way to look on all those passing by him. "Doyle is gonna lose his Kentucky mind when I tell him 'bout this, y'all."

Daddy chuckled and patted Briar on the back.

"Daddy," she said.

"Yeah, baby?"

"Let's go visit Grandpa."

CHAPTER TWENTY-THREE

Hallowed Ground

Briar kneeled at Grandpa Bob's headstone.

"We found out, Grandpa," she said. "Me and Daddy both. Didn't we?"

Daddy nodded. "Yeah, you were right, Dad," he said. "Add this time to all the rest."

Briar's grin faded when she saw a reflection on the grave marker. "What the..."

Trixie peeked around the headstone.

"What are you doing here?" Briar asked.

"One secret I grant ye, but then Trixie must go. Found Lainey, Bob did"—the leprechaun stepped away from the headstone and pointed behind it—"he wanted ye to know."

Briar leaned around to see what Trixie meant.

"Daddy," she waved. "Daddy, come look!"

"What is it, baby?"

Briar pointed at a tin can, its base covered in tinfoil, with a single dinner-plate dahlia growing from it.

"Grandpa." Briar touched the dahlia petals. She glanced up at Trixie. "You've seen him then? And Lainey Grace too?"

Trixie grinned. "In the realm of Ainsley, they run side-by-side. It's often I find them, when we play seek-and-hide. They try and find me, but I's wise and clever. Think they'll ever catch Trixie? I don't. Never."

Briar fought back her tears. "H-he did find her then?"

Trixie nodded. "Bob tells her stories. Lainey knows all of ye here." Trixie winked. "You'll see him again, lass. Of that have no fear."

Then he took off, sprinting through the cemetery before Briar replied.

Briar leaned toward the dahlia, drinking in its flowered scent. "Excuse me, my dear,—"

Briar turned.

Mr. Coldwater stood behind her and Daddy, and the long line of creatures and beings gathering around with them.

"Hope we're not intruding," said Mr. Coldwater.

"No, sir," said Briar. "Just wanted to tell my grandpa what we found out."

"Yes, about that." Mr. Coldwater teetered forward, leaning on his silver cane. "We have come to pay our respects as well."

The old man winced as he knelt to Grandpa Bob's grave and touched his hand to the headstone. "Forgive me, Bob," said Mr. Coldwater. "Forgive me for not coming sooner to thank you for all your years of service to this fine cemetery."

Mr. Coldwater glanced at Briar. "You once told me people

mourn in all sorts of ways and that it wasn't right to lock them out."

"Yessir," said Briar. "That's what Grandpa Bob used to say."

Mr. Coldwater leaned closer to her, his bushy eyebrows raised. "I think Bob was right." He staggered to regain his feet. "From this night forward, I want those gates unlocked and opened wide for any and all who wish to come inside."

Briar jumped up and ran to hug Mr. Coldwater. "Thank you."

"No, my dear," said Mr. Coldwater. "Thank you for teaching me of all the good yet alive in the world. And now—" He stepped away from her, taking a rose from the left breast pocket of his suit and laying it next to the dahlia. "Let us honor this good man who kept these hallowed grounds for so many years. I'm certain my good daughter would not begrudge him some of her roses."

Briar returned to Daddy, taking his hands and wrapping them about her as Mrs. Coldwater and Jesse, Ferd, and all the rest approached Grandpa Bob's grave and laid their roses around the headstone.

Briar stayed in Daddy's embrace long after Ferd and the others said their goodbyes and wandered up the ramp, or else walked out the newly opened gates. They waited 'til Doyle arrived and laughed as Jesse regaled them all with tales of the evening and what the old Kentuckian had missed out on.

Then she watched the media roll in, just as they had every year before then. But once they learned the gates were to be opened ever more, the reporters lost interest in the story and each year thereafter fewer of them showed up until none visited at all.

Not that the roses stopped coming.

Briar visited the grave of Lainey Grace every year when Jesse rang her up to let her know the last leaf of summer had fallen. Then she would ride her old bicycle that she and Daddy fixed together up to the Coldwater mansion and visit the grave with them. Some years they would take roses, others Mr. Coldwater would deliver the newest book in his series, *The Ainslian Tales*, in keeping with his promise.

Briar half-expected the roses to stop after Mr. and Mrs. Coldwater passed away within two weeks of each other. But the following year, the roses arrived again for Lainey Grace and a dinner-plate dahlia for Grandpa Bob.

Every fall was the same, with only the faces of those visiting the grave of Lainey Grace changing—Doyle and Charlene, Jesse and his kids, and eventually even Briar and her own children.

It didn't matter how many years rolled by.

Every fall, when the last leaf of summer fell, roses were laid at the grave of Lainey Grace, and a dinner-plate dahlia on the grave of groundskeeper Robert "Bob" Wade.

And the gates of Coldwater Cemetery remained unlocked.

ACKNOWLEDGMENTS

"People mourn in all sorts of different ways," or so Grandpa Bob would say.

This work is certainly proof of that.

The idea for this story came to me in March 2015. I woke from a nap to the sound of my wife and our oldest daughter laughing outside our home with a family friend. The sun was shining through our bedroom window, the breeze blowing the pink blooms of our crepe myrtle against the glass, and I was mad at myself for having fallen asleep rather than spending time with my family.

And then a thought popped into my head.

Every year, when the last leaf of summer falls, the roses are laid at the grave of Lainey Grace.

Continuing my horrible charade at a work/life balance, I grabbed my computer and off I went into the garden to chase this roses concept. But what I first believed to be a story dedicated to my wife quickly morphed into the story you have just read.

There's a reason for that too.

When I was a kid, I thought my family worked in the death business. Grandpa worked as the head groundskeeper at the cemetery and he had four sons—one a county coroner and funeral home director, another owned the vault company, and all four Galvin boys had worked in the cemetery at one point or another over the years.

Whenever we visited, Grandpa would tell us grandkids to load up in the back of his truck and then we'd go to "help" him lock up the gates in the evening.

In truth, I hadn't really thought much on those times for a long while until this story came to me. Yet the moment I started writing, the words flowed out of me and I pictured myself sitting on the tailgate of Grandpa's truck, hoping to be the first grandkid off the back to reach the heavy, wrought iron gates.

Reflecting on those good times, I realize how privileged I am to not only live among a family of humble caretakers, but to have witnessed their incredible examples of the utmost respect and reverence for both the bereaved and their deceased loved ones.

But this story goes one step further than signifying my want to spend another day with my Grandpa Galvin.

A few months before my wife and I made our cross country move to California in the summer of 2010, my cousin, Adam, at the age of eighteen and only recently graduated from high school, was killed in a car accident. I was in Phoenix on a work trip when I received the news. All alone, staring down a four hour flight home, the "man" in me fought back the emotional side, not wanting anyone on the plane to see some strange guy weeping in Aisle 15, seat C.

And yet, strange as it may sound, I wept for the good memories.

Adam once challenged me to a chili-eating competition and I defeated him by pouring the contents of my bowl into another family member's when Adam wasn't looking, all while urging him onto our next bowl until he ate himself sick. I remembered how Adam had been so proud to drive his new tractor in the local parade...but he forgot to fill it with gas. And though the tractor died on him in the middle of it all, he kept his big grin and chuckled with everyone else.

At some point when we were kids, I gave Adam a nickname: Ferd.

To this day, no one in our family knows how I came up with the name, only that it stuck. The Ferd you read about in this story embodies my cousin, Adam—a drawling voice, a hitch in his giddyup from a stroke he suffered in the womb and then fought against all his life, but most of all, his heart of gold.

People mourn in all sorts of different ways.

This story was my way.

~ ~

Thanks are coming.

First, thank you, dear reader, for sticking with me through this journey.

This story would have never reached you without the support of an amazing team I am honored to be a part of.

I owe Annetta Ribken, more than the three boxes of Kleenexes she has invoiced me for. Much as I believed I had emotion in this story, Netta managed to wring every last drop out of me and push in all the ways only the most amazing editors can. This story would not have been half as good without her patient and guiding hand.

To Jennifer Wingard, who had me in tears telling me how much this story meant to her. Thank you, Jen, for your eagle eyes and saving these readers from what could have been an onomatopoeia struggle bus that I was driving. *Honk! Honk!*

For Valerie Bellamy, and your constant dedication and experimentation to deliver the best work possible. Thank you for yet another gorgeous interior layout and a fantastic conversation filled with laughs when I needed it most.

To the talented Kirbi Fagan, my thanks for the beautifully illustrated cover. I envy your artistic hand.

Greg Sidelnik, you are a port in the storm, buddy. Thank you for always being there to work your graphic design magic and all the conversations in between. You truly wow me every time.

Mom, I couldn't have written this one without you. I don't have enough pages to write how much it meant to me that you would stop whatever you were doing to hear me read new chapters from this story. I love ya.

For Dad, thanks for teaching me how to be a good father, husband, and man through example and for filling in the gaps of my groundskeeper knowledge. (Apologies to my uncles if I screwed up any cemetery, funeral home, and/or vault terms or processes. I promise Dad taught me better.)

To both sides of my family, thank you for not only filling my childhood with stories and laughter, but for teaching me of all the good in life and encouraging me to not just dream, but chase those dreams also.

Last, but never least, thank you to my amazing wife, Karen. I thank you not only for our beautiful children, nor the constant love and support you have shown, but mostly for putting up with my tendency to tackle mammoth obstacles in the midst of life-changing events. I promise this time was worth it.

ABOUT THE AUTHOR

Aaron Galvin cut his chops writing stand-up comedy routines at age thirteen. His early works paid off years later when he co-wrote and executive produced the award-winning indie feature film, *Wedding Bells & Shotgun Shells*. In addition to the Vengeance Trilogy, he also authors the YA urban fantasy Salt series, which is praised for a unique take on mermaids and selkies.

He is also an accomplished actor. Aaron has worked in everything from Hollywood blockbusters, (Christopher Nolan's *The Dark Knight*, and Clint Eastwood's *Flags of Our Fathers*), to starring in dozens of indie films and commercials.

Aaron is a native Hoosier, graduate of Ball State University, and a proud member of SCBWI. He currently lives in Southern California with his wife and children.

For more information, please visit his website: **www.aarongalvin.com**.

Made in the USA
Charleston, SC
22 February 2016